LIFE-DEBT

R.J. BLAIN

Life-Debt
by R.J. Blain

When scavenger and hybrid fox Viva comes across a derelict in empty space, what she and her furry partner, Pandora, discover puts them on a collision course for adventure, fame and wealth—assuming she survives the experience. Teaming up with the derelict's living cargo isn't wise, but the handsome stranger might hold the key to the ship and its many secrets. Add in some pirates out to profit from Viva's living head, and she's in for a wild ride.

Delivering the cargo to its rightful owner is the right thing to do, but getting the job done will test her skills, her sanity, and her limits.

ONE

I went beyond foolhardy straight into the insane category

WHEN IN THE farthest reaches of space, the sane and wise stuck near the shiftgem gates, prayed to whatever entity they believed in, and traveled the most direct route to their destination. The rest risked death straying off the beaten path to venture into the void between the planets, stars, and space stations littering the universe.

I fit in the second category, and I cursed my foolhardy ways while cramming my tail into my spacesuit in preparation for a walk outside my ship. No, I went beyond foolhardy straight into the insane category. Only someone insane headed into the darkest, coldest reaches of space alone.

Well, sort of alone.

Where I went, Pandora followed, all ten, fluffy pounds of her. The red fox, Earth-bred with minor genetic manipulation to increase her intelligence and lengthen her lifespan, made for the ideal companion on long, lonely journeys. Sure, she couldn't speak the primary languages spoken in the explored universe, but she made up for her linguistic failings through being adorable, trainable, and willing to go through hell and back with me for profit.

She preferred her pay in the form of treats, toys, and brushing. I took mine in a variety of currencies, with a preference for galactic standard tokens.

To earn our keep, we tangoed with a derelict that had drifted away from the nearest gate, likely the victim of technical failure. According to my scanners, a few of the derelict's systems worked, and I failed to detect any signs of life aboard the ship. I'd already done the basics for the dead, using the tiny shrine I kept in my cargo bay.

The last thing I needed were ghosts haunting me because I hadn't offered up a prayer for the lost.

With no life to worry about, I could blitz through, grab anything of use or value, and check if their engine still had intact shiftgem crystals. A single pair of crystals, which came in a myriad of colors and qualities, would pay my keep for years. If the freighter boasted a pair of black crystals, I'd be set for life, assuming neither had been damaged.

Without shiftgems, ships couldn't make use of gates, which warped space, time, and distance to allow quick travel between various galaxies without requiring stasis or generational ships. Some still traveled via generational ship, although they were typically reserved for experiments requiring no access to the rest of the universe.

My ancestors, descendants from Earth, had once traveled on a generational ship. Over a thousand years after the start of their journey, I'd been born, a product of their determination to survive. My mother sometimes told me about life on the ship, but she always stated she was glad I'd been born on a tiny, habitable planet in Andromeda. I still questioned how the generational ship had traveled almost three million light years from Earth in only a thousand years.

My mother had shrugged, but she'd given me my first shiftgem shard that day, set in a pendant I still wore.

Until that day, I hadn't realized Earth had been eradicated by the very stones we used to travel between the stars. I questioned how close to human I was, as I shared certain genes with Pandora. My mother claimed I came as close as it got, as I'd been conceived on the generational ship and born shortly after they'd made landfall. Something about her tone, a little sharper, warned me about digging into the little things separating me from my parents.

Neither of them had my ears or tail, a match for my Pandora's. I appreciated having them, however. My ears offered heightened hearing, excellent for planetary exploration. My tail worked wonders for aiding my balance in sketchy situations.

A rather annoying genetic modification involved a tendency to grow a full coat of fur if I stayed in cold temperatures for too long, which shed out after exposure to heat for more than a week. Little sucked more than having to deal with shedding fur on a spaceship.

I supposed my parents, upon being granted permission to have me, had assumed I would need genetic modification for when they made their home on their new world. In reality, the modifications hindered as much as helped.

Inevitably, I lost hours upon hours cleaning filters and vacuuming to make certain I didn't shut down a mandatory system, thanks to unwanted fur floating around when I had gravity turned off in my ship. Fortunately for me, I rarely needed to turn off gravity, as I'd earned a matched set of tri-color shiftgem crystals early in my career as a salvager.

They granted me access to any gate without issue or high risk, powered most of my ship's functions without even a hint of resonance humming, and made me a shiny target for other pirates and treasure seekers.

Well, it would make me a shiny target if anyone knew I had them. As I possessed some common sense and the ability to fix my own engines and gate drive, I had a backup system using a pair of common white shiftgem crystals, which could use a decent number of gates and were often found in exploratory vessels. Anyone without a lot of know-how on the operation of ships like mine would believe the secondary drive operated the entire ship rather than served as my backup. The white crystals couldn't be used to jump often or far without running the risk of resonance or overloading, but their engines tended to zip along at an admirable place.

They could manage faster-than-light travel when set up by someone who knew what they were doing.

As I valued my life, mine could. If my main engine died on me—or my precious tri-color crystals shattered—I could be back online in a matter of hours. In a pinch, I could also move the second engine to another ship.

Like the derelict I meant to board.

Hmm. I'd never tried to haul a dead ship through a shiftgem gate before, but I had a tow assembly, and if I could rig my engine to work with their systems, the large white crystals *could* handle the extra load.

I finished stuffing my tail into my suit and began the tedious process of checking every seam. A leaking seam led to death, and while my suit had come with enough failsafes to please most, life in space had no room for error.

Rather than trust the failsafes, I did a manual check

before running my suit through a base diagnostic scan looking for issues. The oxygen tank, equipped with a tiny green shiftgem crystal, would keep me topped up on oxygen for a period of three hours before I needed to return to the ship to recharge the crystal.

One day, I might understand how a stone could work with technology to circumvent basic science. I struggled enough with the whole idea I could enter the equivalent of an oversized doorway and get yanked across the universe at a rather ridiculous speed.

Chiding myself for allowing my attention to wander to something other than my work, I triple checked the seams before activating the suit's HUD, reading over the diagnostic report. It reported no issues detected. I activated vitals monitoring and crouched beside Pandora, tapping the panel on her suit. While I'd done checks and ensured her oxygen tank worked before gearing up, I pulled up her suit statistics along with her vitals and reviewed them.

She checked out.

"All right, Pandora. Ready to go earn some treats?"

According to her excited squeaking and wiggling of her butt, she was ready to take over the entire universe as long as it earned her a treat.

I grabbed her leash, clipped one end to my belt and the other to her suit. Once on board, I'd activate her magnets, which would allow her to move around on her own, assuming the ship had no gravity. I hoped for gravity. Gravity made my life a great deal easier when plundering a derelict.

"Time to hit the airlock." I waited for the fox to bound forward, the metal pads on her suit clanging against the floor, before following in her wake. As I'd taught her, she stopped in the middle of the square room and sat, waiting for me to close the inner door, flush the oxygen back into the ship, and then open the exterior hatch. The process took less than five minutes, and Pandora waited with admirable patience.

"There's your first treat." I grabbed the ship's main tether, clipped it to my suit, and opened the hatch leading into space. The vast emptiness of the void never failed to amaze me, but rather than gawk at the endless stars, I ran to the edge of the gravity boundary, which ended at my ship's hull, and leapt out, angling towards the derelict.

Yipping her excitement, Pandora followed me.

Upon exiting my ship, I drifted in the direction of the derelict, used a voice command to activate my boot thrusters at their lowest setting, and angled towards the freighter's airlock hatch. I deactivated the thrusters once on the correct trajectory, gave Pandora's leash a gentle tug so she'd alter her direction and join me, and activated my boot magnets, preparing for impact. I collided with the ship, feeling the clang that the vacuum of space otherwise devoured.

Had anyone been alive within the ship, they would've heard me coming long before I could break into their airlock. I twisted, watched for Pandora, and caught the fox. She made two short yips and a bark, activating her magnets, special made to release and activate in set intervals so she could patter around as she wanted. Sometimes, the fox forgot how to use her magnets in her excitement, requiring me to do the work for her. Once I had her secured to the hull, I pressed my glove to the hatch and tested it.

It spun in my hand.

Under normal circumstances, captains locked the

hatches. In an emergency, the wise ones made certain help could get to them without having to break through the airlock. Within a minute, I had the hatch opened, and I clucked my tongue at Pandora. "Bark if there are bodies," I requested.

The fox waited for her magnets to release before beginning her journey to the opening into the ship, careful to pull herself along. After a lengthy stop-and-go journey, she disappeared inside. Moments later, she yipped, her method of communicating there was nothing of interest. I released my magnets and followed her inside, nodding my approval over the pristine state of the airlock. Closing the hatch, I worked to determine if the airlock system remained online.

The lights over the interior hatch activated, and once I pressed the button to gain access to the ship, gravity took hold.

While we'd remain suited for the entirety of our exploration of the derelict, gravity made my job much simpler until it was time to move cargo to my ship—unless I claimed the entire ship as my cargo.

Pandora repeated her double yips and a bark to disable her magnets, went to the interior hatch, and sat to wait for me to give us access. Smiling, I said, "And that's two treats for my best little girl."

Pandora stayed put, although she thumped her tail in general excitement.

Like the exterior hatch, the interior one opened with ease, and some form of gas hissed as it entered the airlock. "Scan atmospheric conditions," I ordered my suit. A moment later, I heard a beep, and the HUD informed me it ran the requested analysis. After a few moments, the report came back with lethal levels of carbon dioxide and other gasses with oxygen levels below the minimum required for life, implying the ship had lost its main oxygenation system somehow.

I wished asphyxiation on nobody, and I murmured another prayer for the dead I'd locate somewhere within the derelict. With luck, they'd be either suited or had already decayed to bone.

The close calls, the ones where if only I'd been a few days earlier, tended to haunt me.

I waited for the hissing to stop before stepping through the hatch and gesturing for Pandora to follow. As I'd taught her, she heeled, and she would continue to do so until I unclipped her leash. Until I got a better feel for the ship, I'd keep her close. After I checked for dangers, I'd turn her loose and give her a chance to shine.

Pandora couldn't use her nose in a derelict environment, but she had an uncanny knack for finding interesting things in odd places.

Once inside the ship, I closed the interior hatch and checked the panel near the airlock, which included a screen display and a full keyboard. Many ships required link access, and while I had the implants installed behind each of my ears, keyboard access implied the designer of the ship had gone the redundant route. Links could fail. Links *and* keyboards were unlikely to both fail except during a catastrophic system shutdown, giving those on board the highest chance of survival.

It amused me that the more expensive systems included older, reliable tech.

I tapped the system access key, and the screen turned on, informing me that the ship's manual override had been activated by the captain. The timestamp indicated the ship had died six weeks ago, and that all members of the crew had gone into their suits to allow for potential recovery of the ship and cargo. Then, in what I counted as a plea I couldn't ignore, he'd left the ship's destination.

Had the ship lasted a few more days, they would have passed through the gate and arrived alive.

In what I viewed as admirable bravery, the captain had given a play-by-play of the ship's final moments, beginning with the breakdown of the main oxygen circulation systems. They had been unable to bring the system back online with no mention of why it refused to work.

To worsen their situation, the communication systems had gone dead during the same event, preventing them from sending word via their crystals, which connected to their destination planet, Cremora Delta 005-26. I recognized the naming convention as something from early human explorers who'd gotten lucky and escaped Earth on faster ships, leaving the generational humans to fend for themselves.

The Cremorans had taken roughly five hundred thousand humans away from Earth, establishing them on a variety of planets named after the Greek alphabet. The relevance of the numbers remained a mystery to me.

I could fix the communication problem readily enough through taking the crystals to my ship and plugging them into my system, reading the origin etchings to retrieve the needed comm code.

"It looks like we're a proper salvage crew today, Pandora. Whatever cargo they have is important enough the captain bothered with setting the ship up to be easy to take. Now, why would he do that?"

Pandora regarded me with her bright eyes and waited

with admirable patience, likely hoping for another treat. Ah, hell. Those eyes got me every time. "And yes, you get a third treat for being so damned cute."

She squeaked at me.

I read through the message from the captain again, tapped on the keyboard to check if their short-distance relay system was online and discovered it worked. I accessed my ship's system and began getting a full dump of the logs to review everything from the comfort of my chair without having to wear a suit.

Then, to hopefully keep the ghosts at bay, I offered yet another prayer along with an apology I hadn't arrived in time to do them any good.

Once the data transmitted to my ship, I accessed the ship's manuals, learning the layout of the place. My eyes widened as I read the labels of the primary rooms, including a stasis chamber. While a foundational piece of generational ships, stasis chambers cost more tokens than I cared to think about, typically required three people to successfully activate, and could turn people into cargo, which explained a great deal about the situation.

My ship lacked a stasis chamber, but I'd invested in a revival system should I happen across any unfortunate soul abandoned in stasis on a derelict. Authorities across the galaxy paid a fortune for the successful retrieval of those locked in stasis, with a bonus for reviving them and aiding with their recovery.

The derelict's chamber was located not far from the airlock, and after a little work, I managed to send a copy of the blueprints to my suit for reference along with the crew and passenger list. A dead captain did me no good, but if someone had been locked in stasis, the nature of my work would change yet again.

I found the chamber, cracked open the door, and discovered three bodies at their posts, with a man of human descent lying on the stasis slab in the middle of the room, the clear dome still in place over him. His pale skin implied a great deal of time flying throughout the universe with little time on planets.

I made a point of going planetside for a month or two at a time to keep from turning into a living ghost, one of the more annoying nicknames land dwellers gave to those of us who spent more time on ships than with our feet on the ground.

The white shirt contrasted enough with his skin I suspected he came from some planet dwelling stock. I'd gotten a decent hit of melanin pigmentation from genetic manipulation.

My parents defined what it meant to be living ghosts.

I needed to return to their new planet sooner than later to visit, perhaps after I got paid for delivering the freighter and its cargo, living and otherwise. If all went well, the journey wouldn't take long.

If all went well.

"Display crew list," I ordered.

The HUD display informed me there had been four members of the crew.

"Display passenger list."

To my relief, there were no names.

All right. From what I could tell from the situation, the crew had loaded one of their own, who likely would need treatment for oxygen deprivation upon revival. Their presence at the monitoring stations implied they'd stood vigil until they'd passed away, one by one. Two of the bodies had slumped over away from the controls, and I took care not to peek inside their suits.

I would not appreciate beholding multiple weeks of decomposition.

The other had slumped to the floor, requiring me to step around him to access the display. In their haste to put their companion into stasis, they hadn't input any of his relevant information into the system. I tapped on the keyboard, reviewing the stasis chamber's log.

In normal circumstances, the process of putting someone into stasis took up to an hour. They'd done the work in under forty minutes, which warned me I might have trouble on my hands reviving him. In good news, the system reported decent general vitals when he'd been put into stasis, which led me to believe he'd been put in before showing symptoms of asphyxiation, an unfortunately long process on a spaceship with some functioning systems.

I questioned if he'd been conscious when he'd been put into stasis, sedated first, or how they'd determined who'd lived and died.

Their system required three people to operate the stasis chamber.

I checked through every file searching for the man's identity before giving up and debating what to do. He'd been put into the case wearing a long, white shirt and nothing else, a standard procedure.

No matter. It didn't matter who the man was. The captain's final message made it clear where he would be going—and I'd do my best to get the ship and the three deceased crew back to their origin planet as well.

The gentleman on the slab would be a problem. First,

I'd have to wrangle him into a suit. Stasis worked wonders on keeping people alive, but if I dragged him out of the ship into the vacuum of space, I'd lower his overall chances of survival by at least twenty-five percent. As such, I would need to stuff him into a space-proof body bag or a proper suit.

I eyed his body, which had been in good physical shape at the time he'd been put into stasis.

Bringing up the ship's blueprint on my HUD, I examined the ship's layout, identifying several utility closets and the crew quarters, which might have something useful for protecting him from exposure to the harshness of space.

I unclipped Pandora's leash from her collar and said, "Guard." To make it clear who I wanted her to defend, I patted the shell of the stasis chamber. With an excited yip, she took a position between the man and the room's sole doorway.

If anything changed, she would bark until I came.

After coiling her leash into a tight loop and securing it to my utility belt, I began my tour, heading for the utility closets to discover what I had to work with. The first few closets contained a mess of spare parts and tools, and someone had scattered everything, likely fighting to fix the ship without a scrap of good fortune. In one of the proper supply rooms, I found several spare suits and bags meant for the injured or those in stasis, allowing for an all-important oxygen tank and the mandatory heaters required to keep the chill of space at bay, both required to preserve life. I checked the oxygen tanks first, determining that the crew had made use of several but reserved two when it became apparent they wouldn't be surviving their voyage. Each tank would last for twenty minutes each, sufficient to get my new guest aboard my ship. I grabbed one and the bag in the best condition and hauled them back to the stasis chamber.

Pandora maintained her post, and I promised her yet another treat for doing as told without reminders.

While smart, especially for a fox, she remained an animal running dog hardware and cat software, which tended to create chaos. Some commands she handled better than others. Once I set her loose to find interesting things, I'd have to leash her to put an end to her desire to explore every single nook and cranny in the derelict.

In good news for the man locked in stasis, the derelict's heaters hadn't completely failed, nor had the vacuum of space yet infiltrated the hull, which would simplify my job. In a way, I longed for the removal of gravity, which would make stuffing him into the bag easier. Unfortunately, it would make checking the bag and the seals harder, along with complicating the process of working with the oxygen tank. I unlocked the shell protecting his body, opened it, and opted for putting him in the bag feet first. He weighed a lot for his size, and I suspected he exercised to escape the monotony of space travel when off duty.

I exercised to maintain my health, and I forced myself to do thirty minutes a day.

It took a lot of muscle and endurance to plunder dead ships of their treasures.

Within five minutes, I had my strangest bit of cargo packed away with the oxygen turned on. Making use of the unlocked console near the airlock, I deactivated the ship's gravity. I checked the display, waiting for any warning lights informing me I would be stuck, but the gravity wells appeared to be in good working order.

Excellent.

I returned to the stasis chamber, snagged the bag by a handle, and began the tedious process of floating him to the airlock, making use of the magnets and thrusters in my suit in equal measure, careful not to damage my living cargo.

"Heel, Pandora."

My fox yipped and barked to activate her magnets and followed me.

As reversing stasis would take more time than I wanted to spend, I terminated gravity in the airlock sector of my ship, yanked the bag off my guest, and left him in the hall, careful to restore gravity when he was on the floor and wouldn't have far to fall.

With one problem out of the way, I headed back to the derelict to explore and discover what other treasures the ship hid.

TWO

While I prided myself on my general ethics, I wasn't dead

THE DERELICT'S cargo bay contained a fortune of shiftgems. Each container listed the type, grade, and number of crystals, if they were part of a set, their order identification number, planet of origin, certification number, and color. I beheld an entire planet's ransom, and I'd already given my word to fulfill the captain's final wish.

Damn.

The second cargo bay also contained even more shiftgems, but it also contained a few engine cores, comm systems, and spare parts so someone could make good use of the wealth of stones ripe for the pickings.

Damn, damn, damn.

With an entire ship full of shiftgems, I might even be able to bring the freighter back online, given the right tools and parts. If I could restore the engine to idle with the gate drive functional, I could limp it to the nearest allied spaceport and turn it in along with the man I'd revive just so I ensured I received some form of payment.

I'd enjoy the process more than I should, but while I prided myself on my general ethics, I wasn't dead, he was handsome, and I'd enjoy the view required to bring him back out of stasis alive.

The idea of checking over his chest and stomach appealed.

I made a mental note to find a half-decent partner in the next spaceport I stopped at for more than a few hours.

With a better idea of what the ship held, why the captain would want his precious cargo returned, and a modified risk factor involving every pirate in space wanting a piece of my pie, I decided to skip straight to the chaos portion of my day. "Pandora, search."

The fox yipped her excitement and began poking through the crates. She vanished into the cargo bay, leaving me to do my own investigating. I grabbed a top-grade box of black shiftgems, which had several sets crystals meant for engine use but would operate just about any system assuming the stones fit the brackets.

At a minimum, I needed to restore the primary engine. If I could get the ship to operate at idle thrust or minimal thrust, I could tow the damned thing to the gate, join the ships together, and jump both simultaneously. With black crystals operating the freighter's engine, it could easily drag my ship along for the ride.

I needed that sort of luck if I wanted to get the freighter back to where it belonged without falling prey to pirates. While my ship could outrun just about anything flying, I lacked much in the way of firepower. I kept some weaponry on board, but it existed to redirect or destroy space debris to make passage safer, not fend off someone out for my head.

The next few days wouldn't be good for my blood pressure.

In the engine room, I discovered a mess of shattered shiftgem crystals. At least three sets littered the floor, and I pegged the blue stone fragments as the one responsible for the loss of the life support system. The brown engine core would cause some issues, as it implied the ship had been a long-distance speed hauler.

The black stones might fit—but they might burn out the engine if the designers had done a shit job with the temperature controls and throttling. I wrinkled my nose, wondering who had thought using brown shiftgems had been a good idea.

Brown stones were meant for farm equipment and construction engines, big, powerful, and lumbering things meant to handle huge loads. Brown in space meant trouble, especially when used on a smaller ship.

Some fucking moron had killed three men for pride and the illusion of better hauling capacity.

I set my box down, headed for the life support system, and eyed the mounting bracket. Whatever had shattered the stones hadn't done any obvious damage to the device. I tested the bracket's movability, the pads for the crystal, and the sensors.

All passed visual inspection.

How odd.

What could have shattered the gems *without* damaging the brackets?

I accessed the ship's systems and scanned for the list of installed shiftgems. After a few frustrating minutes, I located the life support system, recorded the crystal size, and checked the box.

Luck remained with me, and I plucked out the appropriate stone, slid it into the bracket, and adjusted the mounting so the stone would be held in place even when the main engine thrummed to life.

Using the engine room's console, I began a diagnostic scan on the life support system. While it churned through the test, I investigated the other downed systems. I determined the green stone shards had belonged to the water purification system, which could remain offline. The security system, including cameras, sound, and motion detection, were also down and would remain so until someone else fixed it. I set the brackets to the proper empty and locked position, cleaned out a few stray fragments, and moved onto the main problem of my day: the engine.

My first challenge would be finding a set of crystals the correct size. None of the blacks in the box fit, so I hauled them back to the cargo bay and began the tedious process of finding compatible stones. After an hour, I got lucky with a tri-color set in the right size for the engine. I'd have a quirky engine when I finished getting it operational, but quirky beat prone to catastrophic failure.

If it weren't for the brackets being in pristine condition, I would have assumed the brown crystals had exploded, taking out the nearby machines. The lack of actual damage to the parts implied something gentler had happened—like someone taking a hammer to each of the stones and scattering the fragmented ruins across the engine room floor.

The stones might not have even been in the mounts when broken.

That left me with more questions. Who would break the engine and life support systems? Why?

Why lock one man in stasis as a last act of heroism? On

most ships, the saboteur would have been given a quick death to spare dwindling resources, a last-ditch survival effort. The man on my ship had held value to the remaining crew.

Nothing added up.

After cleaning the mounts of shards and crystal dust, I tested the bracket, installed the tri-colored shiftgems, and returned to the console. To my delight, the life support system checked out, and a cheerful green button offered a restart of the system. I tapped it.

One by one, the red warning lights associated with the machine flicked to yellow. As the system churned through its various safety checks, those lights changed to green. Switching to the ship's overview, I navigated to the monitoring systems to check the oxygen levels.

Sure enough, the system began to function again, and the levels of oxygen began to climb to survivable levels while the other toxic fumes decreased.

What the hell was going on? It had only taken plundering the cargo to restore the system. With no evidence of a repair attempt, I came to one conclusion: somebody had blocked access to the engine room while the crew perished, and the saboteur had unlocked the systems in his final moments.

My thoughts skirted into conspiracy-theory territory, but as it was the only idea I had that matched what I worked with, I decided to stick with it. A mass malfunction and mysterious restoration of the system made zero sense.

Someone had meddled, and their meddling had cost three men their lives. If I worked hard, did everything right, and took care with my unexpected guest, it still might cost him his life, too. I would do my best to save him, but I acknowledged my best might not be good enough.

Time, experience, and improved technology decreased the odds of death to one in ten thousand. As long as I reminded myself I had brought hundreds of people out of stasis without losing anybody, I could limit my worrying while waiting for my unexpected guest to resume breathing.

Perhaps he held the answers to my questions.

I began the tedious process of confirming the shiftgem installations before running a diagnostic scan on the engine. Unlike the life support system, the engine began throwing errors left and right, indicating I might have a big repair on my hands. After a few minutes and checking the manual, I determined the problem involved some loose nuts and bolts holding the gem coupling unit to the main drive. One trip to my ship for my toolbox later, I removed the screws to access the main drive core, did some tightening, and reduced the diagnostic errors to one, which involved the shiftgem mounts. Muttering curses, I raided the cargo bay for extra supplies, dug out an entire new mounting assembly, and unseated the gems, returning them to their case for safe keeping until I dismantled the entire engine, replaced the brackets, and put the whole thing together again.

Two hours and much cursing later, I had a functional engine for low thrust with jump drive capabilities.

Excellent.

In the time I'd spent playing mechanic, Pandora had explored, but to my astonishment, she found nothing we considered to be of interest beyond the cargo bays loaded with wealth, not even a single ounce of some recreational drug many space crews stashed in their bunks.

While I typically paid the fox in treats for the number of

illicit goods she found, I promised her an extra treat for being patient. She bounced around my feet in her little suit, the metallic pads clinking against the ship's floor.

For my final trick, I investigated the ship's broken comm to discover yet another set of broken shiftgems. Another search through the cargo bays resulted in a set of yellow crystals, which would be suitable to open communication lines with the ship's originating planet.

I expected a great deal of fun when I activated the system. Linking my suit to the ship's comm, I pressed the activate button, scrolled through the menu of saved contacts, and picked the originating planet's comm officer as the most likely one to get me to someone who could give me coordinates for where to take the derelict. Bracing for a scolding and accusations, I tapped the connect button.

The comm crystals hummed to life, and the machine buzzed. A dark panel on the screen glowed, and I sucked in a breath.

Most spaceships didn't come equipped with voice *and* video communication systems. The crystals and base machine cost too much. Only species who relied on physical modes of communications tended to dish out for them. While the screen remained illuminated but black, a time-delay indication popped up, indicating we'd have a half second delay hampering us. In reality, we'd have to take turns doing full relays, although the lag wouldn't bother most.

We might run into some trouble if we both attempted to talk at the same time.

After a short wait, the screen flashed and pending connection dialog appeared.

"Pandora, heel," I ordered.

Without being aware of what was visible on their end, I would play it safe and keep my companion close to my side.

An older version of the man I'd left lying in the hallway of my ship stepped into the camera view, and his expression went from hopeful to neutral in the blink of an eye. I wondered how long he'd been waiting for the ship to make contact.

Upon consideration, I opted to speak in the most common trade dialects used across the known universe, as most people were taught rudimentary proficiency from an early age. "My name is Viva, and I found this derelict near a shiftgem gate. I would like to return the crew and cargo to its home planet, Cremora Delta 005-26 according to the ship records. Three members of the crew are deceased, and my ship lacks the equipment required to put the bodies into stasis. Their remains are contained in their suits. One member of the crew survived, but he was put into stasis. I *do* have the appropriate training, certifications, and equipment required to restore the individual, although I have not done so yet. I've only just restored this ship to questionable operational status, but I believe I can transport it within range of Cremora Delta 005-26."

"Do you have the identification of the living member of the crew?" the man replied, using the same form of trade.

Phew. Good. One problem solved. With the worry of communicating out of the way, I settled in for the important work of negotiating with the stranger. "Unfortunately not. The ship's logs had a record of four people. I assume the captain is deceased, judging from the messages left. The bodies are in fairly advanced stages of decomposition, and I don't dare break the seals on their suits. As it is, the ship will need to be quarantined. It suffered a life support system failure along with the breakdown of several other systems. I was able to get most systems back online, but it may a while to get the ship to its destination. I will begin the process of decontaminating the member of the crew on board my ship, but we'll need to be in isolation for a minimum period of ten days."

I wrinkled my nose at the thought of sharing close quarters with a handsome man for ten days—one I couldn't put my hands all over due to his classification as cargo.

"An escort will be provided," the man replied. "Was there any cargo on board?"

I nodded. "I required the use of several of your shiftgem crystals to bring the ship back online, but I assumed you would rather lose some crystals and have the rest of the load returned. There are limited shiftgems that are compatible with the engine and other systems. I can't promise they will remain in good condition, although I did my best to match crystals to the drives. This ship used a brown shiftgem core drive, which is the likely culprit. Brown shiftgems are not typically suitable for use in vessels of this size."

I'd leave the whole idea of sabotage out of the discussion, especially if my cargo's father had been loitering in some comm station hoping for word, weeks after hope should have been lost.

"I will make a note to report that. Can you send your coordinates?"

"I can, but please understand that I will begin hauling the derelict to the nearest shiftgem gate as soon as it's possible to travel. This area is not safe. The gems I selected for use in the drive core can handle the jump, and the ship almost made it to its destination."

"Do you have the identification of the shiftgem gate in question?"

I held up my hand to indicate I needed a moment, went to the nearby console, and began tapping at the keys until I was able to pull down the coordinates, which I relayed. "Does this connection allow for data transfer outside of video?"

"It does."

Well, I had nothing to hide for a change, as my ship had been cleaned top to bottom of anything illegal. I hadn't registered my unnamed guest yet, and I wouldn't until I began the process of reviving him from stasis. With no bounties on my head, valid permits for a year, a new captain's license, and a paid-off ship, I could give them all the data they could hope for, including the scans from my ship. "Please open the communication line from your end. I will send over a copy of the scans from my ship before I boarded along with this vessel's logs. This system is a little different from mine," I admitted. "If you initiate the connection, however, I can handle the rest of the transmission."

"Ah, yes. Of course. It's a newer linking system. Are you alone?"

I gestured to Pandora, who remained sitting where I'd asked her. "It's just me and Pandora."

"What species is your companion?"

"She is a *vulpes vulpes*. A red fox. She's an Earth species, with some minor genetic manipulations for survivability and intellect."

His interest piqued, and he continued to stare at my fox. "And she is not modified to a new species designation?"

"She is a certified *vulpes vulpes*."

"Might I ask how you acquired one?"

"I'm *homo sapiens*," I replied, sighing as the ritual of species identifications began. "I was conceived on a generational ship, modified prior to birth for survivability, and born on a planet in Andromeda. Pandora's mother and father belong to my parents, and they gave her to me when she was a kit. She is modified to have an extended lifespan and higher-than-normal intellect. She's a little larger than standard *vulpes vulpes.*"

"And you were modified to have ears?"

"And a tail. They were not certain what dangers would be on the new planet, so I was modified to have an extra pair of ears, heightened hearing and sense of smell, and a lengthened lifespan. The tail was an unexpected consequence of the enhanced genetics for my ears, although it helps with balance. I still qualify as *homo sapiens*, however."

"Impressive. And you said you're originally from Andromeda?"

"That's correct."

"Ah, I see. Yours was the final Earth generational ship to reach its destination planet. You're the last generation of Earth-born *homo sapiens*, then."

It annoyed me that conception on a ship equated to being Earth-born. In a way, I understood the logic, but it meant nothing in the grand scheme.

Earth remained uninhabitable, and it likely would for thousands of years. One day, the catastrophe that had brought the planet to its knees might settle, but I had my doubts. The activated shiftgems once locked in the planet's core had taken over. One day, some enterprising planet buster would head to Earth, blast it to smithereens, and gather the precious crystals to be used elsewhere.

For now, Earth endured as the lost home of humanity, preserved by other species for when it reverted to its blue-green splendor. I admired those who'd welcomed humanity with enthusiasm and warmth.

The first humans to travel the stars had been prejudiced due to ignorance, although change had come, measured in hours rather than years. Do or die had applied, and most had chosen survival over unfounded hatred.

The rest had died with Earth.

Being an endangered species sucked, especially when idiots got it into their heads to issue bounties in an attempt to gain fresh *homo sapiens* genetics into their bloodlines. "Yes, sir."

"Klerano," he replied. "You should be receiving a link request momentarily."

Sure enough, a prompt appeared requesting permission to establish the link. I accepted, and once the ship had the data connection open, I began transferring the ship's log over along with a copy of my scan results from my ship. "The transmission is in progress."

"Excellent. What can you tell me about the damage to the ship?"

I appreciated the transition to a different subject, and I began a detailed description of how I'd found the broken shiftgems and the steps needed to repair the various systems. I mentioned I'd left the water systems offline to minimize the number of crystals in operation in the engine room, recommending a better buffering system be installed, as it was impossible to tell if some form of resonance had shattered the installed gems. I went on to detail how the packing of the stones in the cargo bay would have prevented any potential damage to the cargo if resonance had occurred.

I made no mention of my suspicions of sabotage, nor did he ask for my opinion regarding the derelict's state upon my arrival.

"You mentioned having the ability to revive people from stasis," Klerano prompted.

"Yes." I tapped at the console and added a copy of my medical training and stasis certifications, along with my flawless record of emergency stasis revival. "While I can't put anyone into stasis on my ship, I have the appropriate equipment and training to revive most species from stasis. The process itself takes a few hours, during which I will be closely monitoring the patient. I have everything on board to treat most stasis conditions. Considering the circumstances, it's best to do it on my ship. I don't know what his health was when he was put into stasis, and he may have been suffering from oxygen deprivation when he was put into the machine due to the ship's system failures."

"I take it the ship is still uninhabitable?"

"Diagnostic: life-support system," I ordered my suit, which began a scan of the atmospheric conditions. Within two minutes, I marveled at the system's ability to recover. "The ship is now capable of supporting life, but I'll remain suited for safety reasons. That said, I was able to restore oxygen generation, and the air quality is now survivable. I don't know if the repairs I made will last, and as such, the surviving member of the crew will stay aboard my ship in quarantine."

"You assume he will survive."

"Well, I certainly didn't invest in a half mil token system to lose people reviving them from stasis," I countered.

"Your system was that expensive?"

"Yes, sir. I bought new with every feature I could get my

hands on. I enjoy rescue missions, as they pay well with minimal risks to my ship and myself. I'm paid by surviving recoveries. I'm trained in some systems on how to put someone into stasis, but that is a last, desperate measure—likely what had happened among the crew in their final hours. It appears the crew's last act was to monitor the man who was put into stasis, as I found their bodies in the chamber at the mandatory stations." I hesitated, but then I added, "They now sell a one-man operated stasis chamber, although it's out of my general budget. Also, the shiftgem operating my system was in addition to the revival system itself."

"Would you install one on your ship if you could?"

The number of lives I could have saved, if only I had a stasis chamber, staggered me. "I would sacrifice more than a little cargo space for a stasis chamber, sir. In space, we are all brothers and sisters, and while there are pirates, living bodies are worth more than most corpses. And once in stasis, assuming the victim isn't jettisoned from an air lock for taking up space, they can endure for hundreds or thousands of years. Only space scum settle for murder if stasis is an option. Personally, had I been able to afford one of the new stasis chambers, I would have been able to save far more lives."

I also would have been able to freeze the decaying corpses in their suits to make the lives of those dealing with the deceased a little easier. I forced my expression to remain neutral. But, as he'd asked, I sent along the victim count I'd registered as potentially survivable with appropriate medical care.

"What *is* your profession?"

"I locate and recover derelicts and their crew," I

answered, grateful I could support my claim through additional documentation, which I sent over at the press of a few buttons. "Most would call me a treasure seeker, but if I can return the cargo and crew for a finder's fee, I prefer that over making use of a recovery market. In this case, it's a planetary supply of shiftgems. Morally speaking, my only choice is to return the ship and her crew to your world, even if there isn't a finder's fee."

"You weren't aware?"

"Of what, sir?"

"Klerano is fine, truly. You have earned the familiarity with your acts, both brave and humble."

"Klerano," I replied, wondering what sort of custom I missed, as sir was the universally accepted custom, something non-human species had picked up in some strange homage to Earth in her final days. Gender had managed to get lost in translation along the way, with everyone sharing the same address. In a way, I liked it.

Everyone stood equal. *Everyone.*

It made navigating the universe and its many species much easier.

"Anyway, there will be compensation for your retrieval of ship, cargo, and crew. There has been an active search for the ship for several weeks now."

Well, considering the value and expense of the cargo, I was unsurprised. "I am sorry I plundered crystals to bring the drives and systems back online."

"That is no matter. The ship is also valuable, and you will be compensated for having done the repairs to make her functional again. Would you have an issue consulting with us regarding the drive core?"

"Brown shiftgem drives are better used for farm equipment. They provide too much thrust and general power for a ship of this size. I replaced the drive core with a tri-color shiftgem set, so given some time to properly tune and recalibrate the engine, it might be a viable permanent set. I'll test the engine on the way to your world." I thought about hiding the true nature of my engine, but I opted for honesty, especially as it would back my abilities to handle their freighter. "I have tri-colored shiftgems aboard my ship, and I have a very versatile system. I can access all shiftgem gates, even the higher-level ones most use black gems to traverse." As I had a special set of blueprints just for my custom tri-color engine, I added that to the tally of things sent over to Klerano. "There. That setup is excellent for small sized freighters, too. Any mechanic worth their salt can convert the drive core to function all other systems as well."

"Your cooperation is appreciated," Klerano replied. "Pardon my ignorance, but it is my first time speaking to someone of your profession. Do you have a title of any sort?"

I shook my head. "Just call me Viva. When I left Andromeda, it was before they ranked the first generation of people born on the planet, so I'm registered as breeding stock verified as acceptable for generational ship programs."

"That's significant, Viva."

"It's considered the second lowest tier among the generational *homo sapiens*," I informed him. "I don't have authorization for serving as crew or anything like that on a generational ship."

"It's quite obvious you're qualified. Your success rating for stasis revivals alone qualifies you. Your ability to restore a derelict ship to operational status also qualifies you. If you would like to undergo a proper evaluation upon arrival to

Delta, I would be pleased to submit your application on your behalf and pay the fees."

My eyes widened at the thought of having a full certification and evaluation. At last check, the cost had rivaled that of my entire ship, when new with no used parts.

I'd bought her used and had enjoyed the lengthy process of customizing her from nose to tail.

"That's quite the expense, Klerano. I've looked into the general application fees for the full testing for generational projects."

"You would get all relevant testing, including psionic aptitude, manipulation compatibility, DNA analysis, and general space aptitudes. It's obvious you're suited for space, as you're venturing alone quite successfully. If your ship registration number on these documents you sent is correct, you have quite the history of solo space travel, including the successful apprehension of pirates and bounty hunters—some of which were out for unwed *homo sapiens* such as yourself. And at your age, you're remarkably decorated."

Ugh. Decorations. Every time I brought someone out of stasis, I got a new decoration. I got some form of decoration or another for every ship brought in and towed from the darkest reaches of space, preserving the open travel ways from dangerous debris. "That's truly generous, Klerano. I don't pay much mind to those decorations. I've never actually been to any of the facilities to receive them. I wouldn't have anywhere to put them."

He chuckled. "I will use our data link to show you your collection, then. It's truly impressive. So, back to business. What do you need from us?"

"Very little," I admitted, although one thing came to mind. "If you wanted to make sure space near the shiftgem gate is clear of pirates and other opportunists, that would make my job a great deal easier. With so many of this ship's systems down, getting her through the gate will be challenging enough. I will have to enforce the ten day quarantine period for the survivor on board my ship, but to streamline matters for you, I will bring the purification system online and set her up for remote control, so she will be clean for boarding. I can't do anything for the bodies, but they took care."

"They left their bodies sealed in their suits. Your destination has a purification system, but your efforts would be appreciated to prevent any additional problems."

"Yes, they are still in their suits, likely with shiftgem crystals installed to mitigate the pressure from decomposition. Their suits were in good condition and there is no evidence of leaking at this stage. I would put them in stasis, but this ship requires three crew to operate."

"We can remotely enable the stasis chamber if you can bring it online. We have the staff on hand."

I nodded. "Then I will do my part here, if you can handle remote control of the stasis chamber." I'd heard of such systems, which made the deaths even more tragic.

Had the comm systems remained intact, then all but one member of the crew might have survived.

What a pity.

"I will begin the process of setting up the stasis chamber. The room will have a comm link by one of the consoles. It will be requesting a connection when you arrive. You can leave this communication channel open in case there is a problem with the other console."

"Pandora, heel," I ordered. "Expect five minutes. I will need to deactivate gravity to move the bodies between stasis sessions. Where would you like me to place them during transit?"

"The crew bunks have straps in case someone passes, and there should be body bags large enough to fit the suits. We use the suits for containment and the bags as secondary protection should the suit leak. The stasis system is capable of handling the suit without additional preparation."

I nodded, and without another word, I headed off to handle the unpleasant work of securing the bodies for their long flight home for burial.

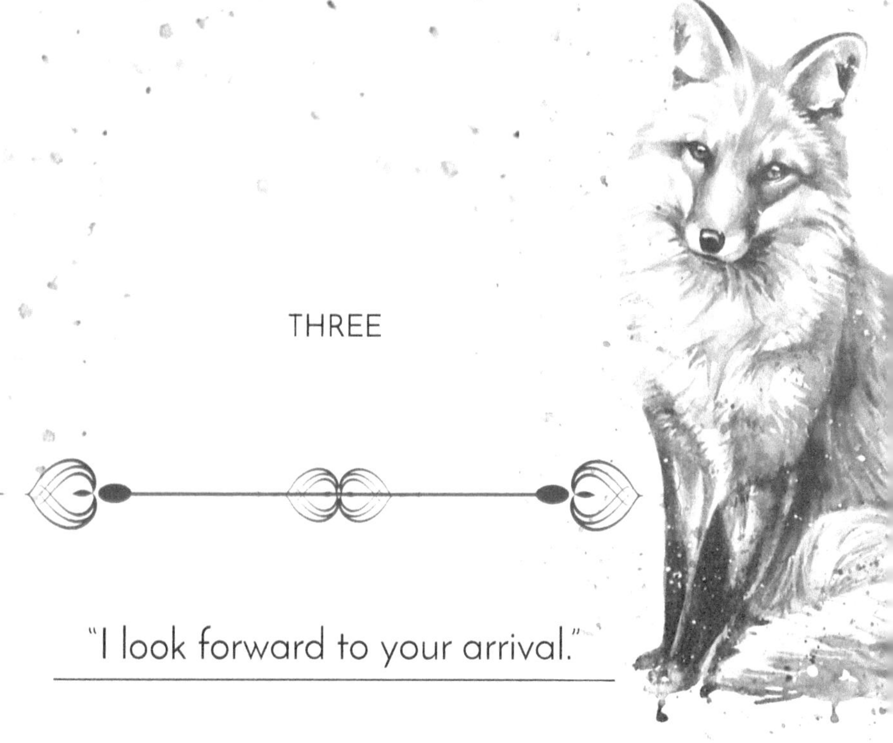

THREE

"I look forward to your arrival."

I SENT Pandora off to explore the ship and attempt to locate anything interesting while I turned off gravity and began the tedious work of putting the corpses into stasis. Without any worries of survivability, the process took less than ten minutes per corpse, and I took care not to get a glimpse at the remains.

I'd seen enough corpses in my lifetime without adding three more to the tally.

Once frozen, I bagged them and hauled them to the crew quarters, strapping them onto the beds for their journey back to their home world. With decomposition so advanced, the bodies would be taken out of stasis while in the suit, and they would be buried as is.

It simplified cleanup.

With the grisly work finished, I reactivated gravity and returned to the main communication room, where Klerano waited with admirable patience. "It is finished."

"Thank you for your service, Viva. It is appreciated. It is

unfortunate the decomposition is too far advanced to identify them."

No wonder. As hope could be a dangerous weapon in the wrong hands, I maintained my silence. If my patient died during revival, I would be able to deliver the news to someone expecting the worst rather than hoping for the best.

Time would tell.

"You're welcome. I will begin the process of towing your ship to Cremora Delta 005-26. I will have defensive systems online, so please have any escort ships initiate contact before coming into close proximity."

"I will make certain that the ships properly identify themselves. You will have a full escort until you reach our spaceport, where you can be docked for quarantine. It's close to our world. We have an excellent quarantining system, so you will be able to receive goods while you wait. It is a day's travel from the shiftgem gate."

I pricked my ears forward at the thought of landing at a spaceport rather than having to go planetside. "Is the spaceport capable of receiving the bodies?"

"When locked in stasis, yes. They have the appropriate equipment. You will be able to unload the freighter in the quarantine bay, which is being prepared for your arrival."

I'd get to make use of an entire quarantine bay? My wallet would cry at the cost of docking my ship and paying the general quarantine fees. "Please send an estimate of the quarantine and docking fees," I requested.

"Paid in full as part of your compensation. You wouldn't need to quarantine if you had not taken it upon yourself to recover the living member of the crew. I will send over the complete compensation report, including the standard taxes and fees, which will be managed on your behalf and certified."

I smiled at that. "Thank you, Klerano. I expect, if all goes well with the towing operation, to reach the spaceport within two days at most."

"I look forward to your arrival."

I disconnected the communication link, heaved a sigh, and ordered my suit to run a new diagnostic scan, which informed me the ship had fully restored its life support system. I called for Pandora, and the fox bounded over, yipping her excitement.

Ah. She must have found something. Excellent. "Show me," I ordered before praising her for her good work and promising a treat for her effort. She bounded off in the direction of the cargo bays, diving into the smaller bay and wiggling through the boxes, some of which had been shifted due to the removal of gravity. She stood on her hind paws, hopped, and yipped several times, indicating someone had stashed something of interest higher up the stacks.

Clever fox, having taken advantage of the removal of gravity to investigate out-of-reach places. I disabled gravity again and used my thrusters to get above the cargo. Pandora joined me and used the boxes to propel herself across the bay. Once near a wall, she activated her magnets, pointed her nose at a box, and yipped to catch my attention.

One day, I might understand how the fox found interesting things when she couldn't smell anything outside of her suit, but she rarely failed me. Sometimes, her failures were the correct identification of boxes containing delicious, tasty treats she loved. I praised her for those finds, as I had told her to find treasures.

Sometimes, she interpreted that as a demand for increased pay.

I patted boxes until she stopped yipping, her cue that I'd found what she'd wanted me to investigate. I checked the sides of the box, discovering a strip of tape wrapped around it, which set it apart from the rest of the crates.

How fascinating.

I grabbed the box, tucked it under an arm, and made use of my thrusters to return to the floor. Once Pandora joined me, I set her discovery on the floor and restored gravity. A few minutes later, after some cursing and elbow grease, I popped the lid off.

The familiar and unwanted sight of a shipment receipt issued from one of the nastier black markets rested on top, and someone had made notations on who was to receive the contents, which consisted of a selection of shiftgem pendants and other stones. The receivers, judging from the method of listing them, were not associated with legal channels. If the crystals had been mined the regular way, they wouldn't have been on the black market, instead selling for a premium at jewelers.

The black market inventory declared the stones to be core shiftgems from pirate-operated planet busting, coming in a full range of colors. Unlike the traditionally mined stones, the pendants could also amplify latent psionic abilities, and in the wrong hands, power the same sort of weapon that had resulted in the acquisition of the cursed crystals.

If anyone found out the ship contained core shiftgems, it would become a nice, juicy target worth more than I cared to think about.

"Good work, Pandora." I repacked the box, including

the inventory slip, and did the only thing I could: I took it with me.

Perhaps I might be able to learn the secrets of the cargo on my ship—and why three men had died over it. More importantly, I needed to identify if the man in stasis was friend, foe, or unfortunate victim of greed, the one trait uniting all species.

AFTER RETURNING TO MY SHIP, stripping off my gear, and detoxing in the fumigation chamber along with Pandora, I went to work preparing to haul the derelict and its cargo to the spaceport, where I could wash my hands of it. A good smuggler created hiding places difficult to access and harder to spot. Aware the core shiftgems would be the target of government officials and pirates alike, I spent the five hours required to dismantle part of the engine, lift up the floor, hide the pendants, and restore everything. While I did the work, I checked over each and every piece of my engines, triple-checked my shiftgems in their mountings, and reported my activities in the log.

In a twist of good luck, I needed to replace three common pieces, which had shown signs of wear and tear.

I made a note in the file that the derelict's engine failure had prompted a safety check, something nobody would think twice about. Anyone with a single grain of sense in their head would've done the same. Once accomplished, I headed for my medical room, which held my revival equipment. After an hour of preparation, I temporarily deactivated gravity so I could move the man into place without breaking my back.

With gravity restored, I checked to make sure nothing had been broken or damaged, put an oxygen mask over his mouth and nose to assist with potential oxygen deprivation, prepared the IV with the appropriate medications to improve his chances of revival, and picked up my prized revival unit, which contained a clear shiftgem. While it wasn't technically a core crystal, mine came close, from one of the deepest mines in the universe.

In reality, most classified it as a core shiftgem, as it had come from the appropriate layer in the planet to possess some unusual properties.

In my hands, it increased the survival rating of revival patients.

I'd received it as a gift for one of my rescues, worth far more than the token fee I otherwise would have received for the unexpected rescue of a diplomat. It remained one of my true treasures, and one of the reasons I held such a good revival success rating.

I sent out a prayer to any benevolent deity that might be listening that the man would revive without complications.

I placed the device over his heart, connected the unit to the chest pads, and pressed the green button, which would begin the process to reverse stasis. The device, as bodily functions resumed, mimicked the pattern of a regular heartbeat. I observed the machine monitoring his vitals, and ten minutes into the process, the computer reported his heart resumed beating and he drew breath.

I sighed my relief at the evidence he would survive stage one. With blood flow restored and his heart beating, I inserted the IV and began phase two, which involved giving him a dose of a medicinal cocktail designed to prevent a series of complications, including stroke, heart attack, and seizures.

The entire time, I kept an eye on his vitals, which reported an acceptable blood oxygen level and stable heart-beat matched with the revival unit.

The moment of truth would be with the removal of the unit, which would allow his heart to beat without intervention. An hour after beginning the process, I turned off the device, tensing while waiting for the monitor to show me the changes in his heartbeat. After several erratic beats, his heart worked on its own, leaving me with the final stage of the process, which involved reversing the sedative used with stasis.

Those who entered stasis unconscious enjoyed a higher chance of revival.

As I had no idea how much of the sedative the crew had used, I began with minimum dosage, administered it, and waited the prescribed ten minutes for a reaction before administering the next incremental dose. After six doses, I began to worry.

The seventh bore fruit in the form of stirring, beginning with eye movement and subtle shifting of his body on the table. I settled in to observe, keeping an eye on his vitals. All remained steady.

Three hours later, my living cargo blinked, revealing rich brown eyes, which would need at least another hour to focus properly. If all went well, coherency would return within twenty minutes, although he'd twitch for the next twelve hours as his nerves misfired and the remnant side-effects of stasis eased.

"Try not talk yet. You're at risk of biting your tongue

right now," I stated in my most authoritative voice. "I recovered you from your ship, and you've survived revival from stasis. In twenty minutes, I'll give you some water and see how that goes. For now, you need to keep still. You were given a high dose of the stasis sedative, and the reversal drug needs time to eliminate it all. I used minimal dosage to prevent long-term consequences of revival."

While he struggled to move, he managed to lift his right hand in an acknowledgement of my words.

"My name is Viva, and I'll be taking you to a spaceport near Cremora Delta 005-26. I don't particularly care what your name is. As far as I'm concerned, you're living, breathing cargo I need to transport along with your ship, so I'm going to call you Delta. I am regretful to inform you the rest of the crew perished. I was several weeks late in locating your vessel, which had suffered through catastrophic shiftgem failure, likely due to the brown crystal drive core. I have since done repairs to the ship, but it is uninhabitable until detoxified. We'll also be required to undergo a minimum of ten days of quarantine. The quarantine period has already begun, and I have been assured we will have a quarantine bay upon arrival at the nearest spaceport, approximately fifty hours and a single jump from here. I'm certain you will have questions, and once you pass your basic health checks, I'm happy to answer them for you. In the meantime, try to relax as much as you can."

With my speech out of the way, I began removing the excess pads from his chest for the revival unit. Applying the alcohol-based rub to remove the glue residue tested me more than I liked, especially as the revival twitching confirmed he spent a great deal of time maintaining his physical fitness.

In any other situation, where he wasn't the equivalent of cargo and a patient, he would have tested me in more ways than one. I would regret the circumstances of our meeting for quite a while, however.

It took work to find a compatible male to have an energetic dalliance with when traveling the great empty reaches of space.

Twenty minutes later, he passed his health checks, and I helped him sit up so he could drink. "I'll leave the IV in for another twenty minutes in case you have an adverse reaction, but at this stage, you should be fine. If you try to talk, do so with care. Your tongue might still be stiff or twitchy, and I don't have a supply of blood should you injure yourself, Delta. Try not to be too offended. I don't do the names thing much."

"Yet you told me your name is Viva," he replied in a raspy voice.

"She who drives the ship can do what she wants," I countered.

Rather than become annoyed, as most tended to do when I made it clear I had boundaries while on my ship, he chuckled. "You dodge attachments with your cargo, I see. Delta's fine. Your ship, your rules, and that's not an unreasonable rule."

That simplified matters. "Precisely. What do you remember before you were put into stasis?"

"Very little. The ship had a life-support system failure, which we weren't able to repair. None of us had any knowledge or training in repairing shiftgem systems, and the ship lacked tech manuals on how to replace the crystals."

What in all that was holy and pure was a four-man crew doing venturing through the far reaches of space without a competent shiftgem mechanic? "And your stasis system requires three people to use."

"The captain had us draw lots so one of us might get out alive. I drew first, but I got lucky, so I went into stasis. The ship's life support system had an hour left on the clock when I went in. Our suits run on a two-hour tank, but we only had one each of those. The spare tanks are twenty minute tanks. We tried everything we could to bring the alternative systems online, but without knowing how to install and calibrate the shiftgems, we were stuck. If the comm system hadn't failed, things would be different."

That explained a few things; once in the stasis chamber and the first twenty to thirty minutes of the process was completed, the rest of the procedure required little monitoring. The patient would either live or die. The crew had spent their final moments observing and waiting for their oxygen to run out, likely sending out some unheard prayer for salvation that would come weeks too late. "Still, I'm sorry. You were the sole survivor."

"Surviving was more than I expected, truth be told. We only had rudimentary training using the stasis machine. Enough to turn it on and use it, but that's it." Delta's eyes focused on my ears. "May I inquire about your species designation?"

"*Homo sapiens*. I'm modified, but not enough to count as a different species. Yourself?"

"*Homo sapiens Cremora-Delta*. My home world was settled by the earlier groups of *homo sapiens* to leave Earth, and we generally keep to ourselves. We're still biologically similar to standard *homo sapiens*, but we have sufficient genetic differences to have our own designation now. We had a batch of three generational ships, and we were accompanied by the

Cremorans. We still have close relations with the Cremorans, although we aren't a compatible species. We have interbred with the Veloc, although genetically, any humans who enter a relationship with a Veloc have children with Veloc genetics. Sometimes they have *homo sapiens* children, but it's uncommon." Delta rolled his shoulders, wincing. "Is this soreness normal?"

While certain species had tried to intermingle on a romantic level with *homo sapiens*, when a species took in a non-compatible species, it was assumed they either wanted to earn a better reputation or gain a new labor force. The various universal labor groups did a decent job of containing the worst of the labor issues.

Slavery happened, but those enslaved had been given a choice: death for their crimes or a life of forced servitude. When planets indulged in enslavement beyond those terms, several of the labor federations tended to strike swiftly and with great prejudice.

Homo sapiens were a common target of slavers.

Rather than dwell more on the bleaker realities of society, I focused on my more immediate problem: my cargo, who already showed discomforting signs of being a decent conversationalist to go along with his severe case of handsome. "Yes. Being sore is normal. You've been in the same position for several weeks, and while stasis prevents death, it doesn't change that your muscles haven't been used for an extended period of time. What is your originating planet?"

Mostly, I asked to confirm what I already knew, but he wouldn't find that out from me.

"Cremora Delta. You?"

"I was conceived on a generational ship, although I was born in Andromeda. My ears are a survivability trait."

Pandora, who had taken a guard position by the door, yipped. I gave the fox my attention, and she let loose a series of yips, indicating she would like to go use her bathroom. Chuckling, I reached over, grabbed one of her treats, and tossed it for her. "You're off-duty."

She snatched up her treat and ran off to use her litter box and play, likely destroying one of her newer toys or indulging in some extended cuddle time with her favorite cuddle-buddy, which was shaped like a Veloc. Most days of the week, the race reminded me of feathered dinosaurs with big teeth and even bigger claws. I had no idea how a human and a Veloc could reproduce, but after the first few times of trying to figure it out, I decided it involved one hell of a brave person and a patient and gentle predator.

Adult Veloc tended to be an average of eight to nine feet tall, excluding their crest feathers.

I also wondered why humanity had gone with a generic name when everyone else had wisely named their race after their originating planet, thus joining the universal trend of species names being capitalized while humanity waddled along at the back of the group.

Then again, most races had an edge on the average human in size, base intellect, and strength, and most branches of humanity went out of the way to master the art of bioengineering to survive among the more cunning races.

Like the predatory Veloc.

Delta grimaced again, shifted his weight on the table, and began the long and painful process of getting his body to cooperate. I waited, as I'd learned any commentary tended to agitate those struggling to recover from stasis revival. After what felt like an eternity but was closer to ten minutes, he gestured towards where my fox had stood guard. "What sort of animal was that?"

"She's a *vulpes vulpes*, commonly known as the red fox. She's slightly modified for a longer lifespan and higher intellect. She's my partner. Her name is Pandora. My generational ship received the fox as our companion animal, as we were the last generational ship to depart and the other ships had first crack at animals." Other ships had gotten dogs, horses, cats, or other companion species, but we'd gotten the one of six wild animal species determined to be suitable for the rigors of space. They'd thrived, and a careful breeding program had kept them close to their Earth equivalent.

Unlike Earth's foxes, Pandora might live to be fifty to sixty years old—maybe longer if I invested extra money for genetic rehabilitation as she aged. Knowing me, I'd invest every token I could to keep her with me until the day I died. From there, I could only hope someone would take over my role as her caretaker and companion.

"Her tail and ears are much like yours."

I nodded. "Our generational ship only had the *vulpes vulpes* as our extra animal. We had mice and rabbits and similar animals in the conservatory, some of which were bred to be prey for our foxes. I suppose my ancestors spent their time working on viable genetic manipulation to improve the fox, and then took the good traits, like their hearing, and manipulated the final generation conceived on board."

"Like you."

Bobbing my head, I went through one last round of checking the equipment before freeing him from the remaining cables and sensors. "You're going to feel unpleasant for another day or two. It's completely normal.

You'll require light physical therapy, which I'll guide you through during our mandatory quarantine period."

"Why are we quarantining?"

"There's no way of knowing if your ship was contaminated with three corpses on board. It's standard protocol, especially with mixed species. As you aren't my same species and we may not share equivalent vaccinations, we'll have to undergo treatments if we infect each other with passive viruses."

Delta's eyes widened. "I hadn't realized that was a possibility."

"Usually, mixed species aren't quarantined, but as there were corpses on board your vessel in advanced stages of decay, we have to follow the rules for those with compromised immune systems. As you are suffering from stasis revival, your immune system *is* compromised and will be for the next three to five days. In both good and bad news for you, I'm qualified to administer base post-stasis vaccinations, which I will give to you tomorrow."

"Stasis impairs vaccinations?"

"It disrupts some vaccinations, yes. The immune system has a tendency to wipe the vaccination out during the revival process, and some of the revival medications are known to impair the longevity of certain vaccines. In any case, the vaccinations I carry are suitable for all branches of *homo sapiens*, so it will be no issue."

"Are you a doctor?"

I shook my head. "I'm nothing so special. I just prefer to save lives than take them, and the certifications for stasis revival match well with derelict investigations. Your crew, may they rest in peace, did as a good crew does in the face of such disasters. They save who they can."

"If only it had been a one-man system," Delta murmured.

If only. "I suspect the ship will be overhauled to have such a system in the future. And, perhaps they will finally crack a system allowing the stasis process to be completed by the person in the chamber. That would be complicated, though."

"Because of the sedation."

I nodded. "I am concerned you were given a higher dose of sedative than typically prescribed, but I will monitor you for the next twelve hours."

"Without equipment?"

"Without equipment. It's better to observe you directly. Now, let's try to get you moving around. I can't promise more than a standard jumper, but I have clothing you can wear. I always keep a range of apparel in case of live recoveries. Once you are through the full process, I will open my communication system to your home world."

Delta's eyes widened, "You have a long-distance comm?"

I grinned. "Would you like to see my system?"

"I'd love to. I've always been interested in the drives and shiftgem setups, but I never qualified to become a mechanic."

Pft. In space, qualifications made no difference. Knowledge won the battles and wars against the void. "Well, that will make the next ten days pleasant enough for you. On my ship, you need no qualifications to learn beyond respect for my equipment and a willingness to be taught. So next time, when disaster strikes, you might be the difference between life and death."

"How long do you think it will take to repair my ship?"

"I've already repaired your ship. Once I had the stones from the cargo bay and fitted them, it didn't take long. It was more of a matter of knowing how to do the work without breaking the system. Some of the equipment needed actual repairs, but it was mostly a shiftgem issue."

"The crystals all shattered at once, with a great, thundering roar that reverberated through the ship," Delta said, his expression distant and his eyes unfocused. "And none of us knew if we could just take out the old gems and put new ones in, and we didn't know how to find the right gems for the job."

"You couldn't just take out the old gems and put in new ones. You had to match size and type—or understand which types could stand in. It won't change the past, but perhaps what you learn will change the future."

It wasn't much, but it was all I could offer the man who faced the grief of having been the one left behind to survive.

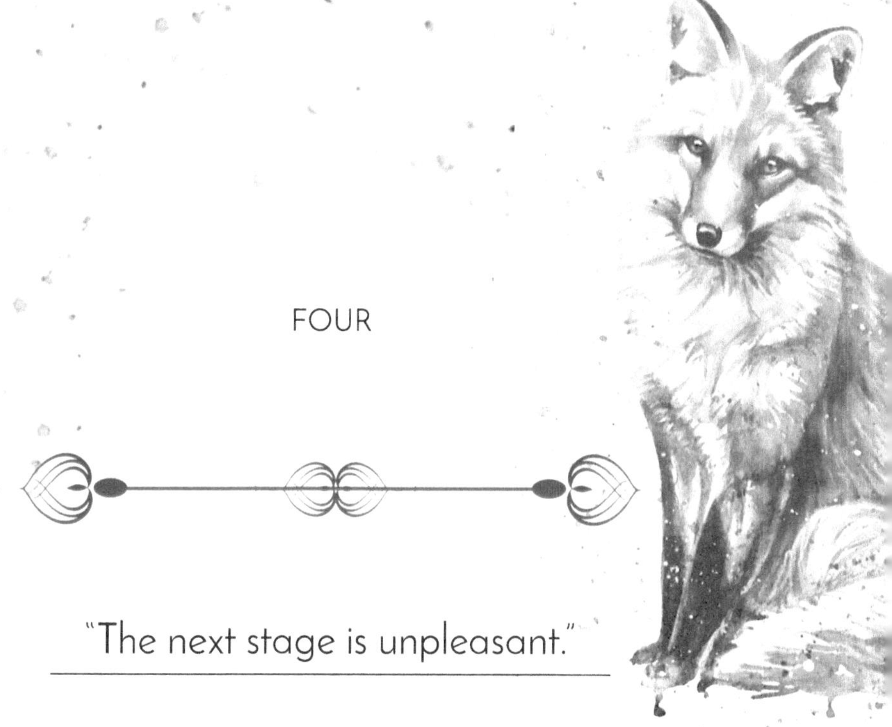

FOUR

"The next stage is unpleasant."

DELTA NEEDED my help to walk, and I admired how he handled going from fit and healthy to reliant on some strange woman with ears and a tail to reach our destination, which was my spare cabin he'd use for the duration of his stay. He heaved a sigh at the realization he needed my help to wipe his skin clean of the stasis residue, most of which he'd sweated out during the twitching phase of revival.

I took care of most of the work, and I chuckled and turned around so he could address the more delicate matters on his own, making use of one of the several solution-soaked cloths I'd provided for the task. Once he'd cleaned to his satisfaction, I assisted with the dressing process, dressing him in one of my spare jumpers. While not ideal, it fit, it would keep him warm, and he could change into something better later.

"The next stage is unpleasant," I informed him once he was dressed and able to stand on his own.

"I wish I had paid more attention to the revival process

for stasis," Delta admitted in a rueful tone. "It's worse than I imagined. How can this possibly become more unpleasant?"

"You have to stand and walk around for at least an hour before trying to eat. While your bodily fluids are thawed now, you need to move around. Once you've moved around, I'll try you on something bland to see if you're ready to eat. Depending on your symptoms, I may have to hook you to an IV, but that's uncommon. To provide a distraction, I'll teach you how good shiftgem systems work. Would you like to learn about the life support system, the engine, or one of the other systems first?"

"Can we start with the revival system? I've never seen one, and I mistakenly failed to pay attention to the classes before departure."

In his situation, with a three-man system and low odds of being the one to go in, I couldn't blame him. "We absolutely can. Most are only given a short briefing on what to expect if revived from stasis, so I doubt your education was all that expansive. I didn't check to see if your ship had a revival unit. Mine does, but I don't have a stasis chamber. That will likely be my next acquisition, assuming I can get the funding required. The revival unit was expensive enough."

Until he could walk without swaying, which would take another few hours, I would keep a firm grip on his arm. While I could deactivate gravity with the link implants, I preferred to keep my ship's secrets close to my chest and nestled up my sleeve in case of a true emergency. We made it back to where I'd revived him, which wasn't much more than a utility closet filled with medical supplies. The revival unit itself counted as tiny but fierce, with the clear shiftgem crystal having cost a whopping quarter of a million tokens.

Its status as a gift was the only reason I had it.

I set the unit on the table, and as I checked the device over after every use anyway, I decided to begin his education with a top-level shiftgem. "This is an upper-level revival unit, meant for portable usage. Most larger ships and ports have full-body cells, similar to what is on your ship. However, those have certain downsides. While cheaper to install, they don't allow the operators to take a hands-on approach with their patients. When I revived you, I had full access to your body in case of emergency."

"That seems important."

"It's part of why I have a perfect record of reviving stasis patients in space. At this stage, if you were to prematurely expire on me, it would not be due to revival itself; some underlying health condition would be the primary culprit. If you have an underlying health condition, now would be the time to tell me."

"I have allergies to certain insects on my home world, but that's it."

"Then you'll probably be fine. So, this unit uses a clear shiftgem crystal. The replacement cost is a quarter of a million standard tokens, so I strongly recommend against breaking it."

At my encouragement, he sat on the table, and once positioned, he raised his hands. "I will look and not touch for the moment."

That worked for me. I placed the unit beside him, opened the protective casing, and exposed the shiftgem and its mounting brackets. "Most shiftgems use a quartet of mounting brackets, although drive cores may use up to twenty depending on the size of the crystal. Each gem would have an equal number of mounting brackets. When the crystals are paired, the stones are cut to be the exact same shape and size, allowing for less than a millimeter of variance. In most systems, the sets can handle up to two millimeter differences, but when you are in space, you can't afford problems. Mismatched sets tend to explode under certain circumstances."

"The captain knew about that, and the stones were in sets. He had no idea what the thresholds were."

"He did the smart thing, then, because a mismatched set can completely destroy your engine." I eased the brackets away from the clear stone and removed it, holding it up for him to admire. "Clear stones of this quality are exceptionally rare, and they're typically core stones taken from active shiftgem planets. Treasure seekers go to the planet when it is at its most volatile and make exploratory trips to capture shiftgem ejecta from volcanoes. Revival unit stones, like this one, are sold at a fraction of the price."

"Is that a core shiftgem?"

I nodded, and I replaced the stone into the brackets, explaining how to secure the gem and test it was mounted correctly. Once done, I returned the unit to its shelf, pulled out the locked metal case carrying its certification paperwork, and opened it. I held out the crystal's identification. "This is a legal stone, taken as a salvage op from an intact planet. I do not condone core shiftgems from busted planets."

"Nobody with a scrap of sense or morality does," Delta replied, reading over my certificate. "This is an Earth core shiftgem?"

I shrugged. "*Homo sapiens* from the generational ships get first crack at them, and I'd done a chain of successful revivals on inferior equipment, so I was offered the stone."

In reality, the gem had been recovered from the final flight from Earth, having been mistaken to be a simple quartz crystal taken from a deep mine. It had ventured for over a thousand years in space before being evaluated as a shiftgem crystal of unusual clarity and unmatched color—or lack of color, as the case was.

"This is worth far more than a quarter million tokens."

"It was onboard my parents' generational ship, and nobody knew what it was. And anyway, it made its way back to me as a gift following a rescue. I couldn't afford a stone of this caliber."

"That's your heritage and birthright, then. How many others from your generational ship venture into space?"

"Very few." To be specific, there was one: me. Everyone else had stayed happily nestled on their new home world. I'd left for training in space at the age of twelve.

By the time I'd turned five, everyone had realized I longed for the stars. I'd been the last to figure it out but the first to embrace the reality of the situation.

I'd been born to fly.

"Earth is quite the valuable shiftgem planet," Delta stated, and he handed the card back. "That crystal alone would make you a prime target among pirates. The entire planet is essentially one giant mass of shiftgem material. It's the planet's primary mineral."

"Is it?"

"It is. The last resource scan puts Earth at having a thirty-five percent composition of shiftgem minerals, with high-grade material estimated to be up to fifteen percent. It's under constant surveillance and protection from planet busters wanting to profit from Earth's destruction. It's estimated at least five percent would be usable core shiftgem material."

I grimaced at the thought of Earth being blown to smithereens to induce the conditions necessary to melt the mineral and allow it to reform into viable shiftgem crystals, which could be cut into the appropriate shape and sizes.

Mine had come in its natural crystalline structure, a double-pointed spear. "I see you're interested in the manufacture of shiftgem crystals."

"I was onboard to negotiate for our cargo, handle base inspections, and check the certifications of all the gems to make certain they're legal. I inspected all the crates upon entry, and I registered them into the ship's log."

Interesting. His statement implied he had no idea about the additions to his cargo bay. Hidden at the top would make the most sense if a smuggler hoped to sneak the box off the ship upon arrival.

It had been of small enough size to tuck into a bag of personal items without drawing attention.

"Well, I'll apologize for making a mess of your inventory, then. I used a few of the crystals to bring your ship back into general operation. I already notified your home world of their usage, and they approved it."

"I would have approved the usage as well, so that's not a problem."

"May I inquire what sort of gems are on board? I will be bringing your ship's engine back to life after you're better recovered from revival so we can head to the gate."

"It's just a shipment of standard shiftgems, nothing nearly as impressive as your core crystal," he replied. "I've never actually seen a core crystal up close."

I grinned at his wistful tone, retrieved the revival unit,

and freed the gem from its brackets. "I don't really consider it to be a core crystal, although it is registered as one. It came from a deep mine, though. Hold your hands out. This one has no history of waking latent talents, but it's something to behold, isn't it? I'll support your hands. You won't drop or damage it."

Delta's eyes widened and he cupped his hands together and held them out. I placed the shiftgem into his hand and closed his fingers around it. "There. Now you can say you've held a core shiftgem. The core gems work best in revival units. My theory is they are the core of life of a planet, so they work best in machinery meant to restore life."

"That's one of the better theories I've heard," he admitted. "Thank you for letting me hold it."

Once he opened his fingers, I reclaimed the gem. Then, as he wanted to learn and I doubted he could do much damage to anything in his current condition, I had him replace the stone in its mount, secure the brackets, and test that the device worked. "There you go. You've now done your first shiftgem installation."

"It was so easy," he murmured.

I expected that reality would hurt him for a long time—assuming, of course, he had any sense of morality. "It took me a lot of work to repair the engine and life support system. It wasn't just a matter of popping in new stones. I had to get replacement parts out of your cargo bay, install and test them, and then install the gems and bring the systems back online. If no one on board knew how to do a proper bracket replacement, you never would have been able to get those systems operational."

"Nobody knew."

"It wasn't your fault. But while I can't erase your guilt, I *can* teach you how to do the repairs once we're in quarantine at the spaceport. We'll have around eight days and a whole lot of nothing to do, so there's no reason I shouldn't dismantle my auxiliary systems and do a very thorough parts check. I just did some work on the engine in a moment of paranoia after returning from your ship and replaced some worn parts. I bet I can find others that could use repair. You can earn your keep while learning how to make certain there isn't a next time."

"I appreciate that. I truly do."

"You might not when I'm finished with you," I warned.

TWO HOURS into torturing Delta with a tour of the ship and showing him the various systems, Pandora bounded over with her favorite ball in her mouth. Her tail whipped side to side, and she writhed in her general excitement.

I hadn't even agreed to play with her, but the amount of energy she expended on the hope I would throw the ball secured her place as the ruler of my life. As usual. Laughing, I crouched and held out my hand. She gave me the ball and bolted for the hallway.

I flung it down and against the wall so it would bounce every which way, providing her with maximum entertainment.

"She has trained you well, I see."

"She's earned it. She did a great job on your ship, and while I already paid her in treats, she knows she gets the ball afterwards as well. I also trained her to be careful during revivals, so she won't ask for her ball until I am no longer heading into the revival room often."

"Quite intelligent, too."

Pandora bounced back, but rather than carry the ball in her mouth, she batted it along the floor, much like an excitable cat. I intercepted her toy and flung it down the hallway again.

"She's very smart. That can be a double-edged sword, but given twenty minutes with the ball, she'll be tired out and be ready for her grooming, her dinner, and some sleep. You can play with her if you'd like. It's good exercise for you."

Delta grinned. "You don't mind?"

"I don't mind at all. Pandora, bring your ball."

The command got her to carry it in her mouth and sit in front of me as I'd taught her. "Delta, hold your hand out for the ball and ask her to give it to you, please."

He obeyed, moving better than most did at his stage of revival. Still grinning, he said, "Please give me the ball, Pandora."

While not the way I phrased it, the fox obeyed, and her bushy tail swished in her general eagerness to resume playing. Rising to his feet, Delta bounced the ball against the floor, resulting in chaos and a happy fox. "Oh, that bounced more than I expected."

"Don't worry about it. Just about everything is secured for when I shut down gravity, and she won't chase balls into the engine room or other delicate system rooms. Play with her however much you like. In the meantime, I'll start preparing the ships for transit. You're out of the danger zone, although I won't depart until I feed you and you're lying flat in your cabin. After playing with Pandora, I expect you'll be exhausted."

"I already am."

I waited for Pandora to bring Delta her ball and him launching it as far as he could to say, "You'll be all right, but if you have any problems, I'll turn off gravity to make traveling to your bunk easier."

"I appreciate that."

"You're welcome."

With fox and man occupied, I began with a system check of my engine before heading into my control room to interface with the other ship. Remote controlling a freighter took work, but I'd done it enough times the process bored me, requiring several checks before I was willing to engage the system and test the engine I'd repaired.

I brought up the video surveillance of the ship on the screen, and almost an hour after leaving Delta with Pandora, I checked on the pair to discover them sitting on the hallway floor engaging in a game of catch the hands and paws.

Typical Pandora, charming every sentient foolish enough to fall into her clutches.

"I'm about to bring your ship back online and start the engines if you'd like to observe. I don't know if you have any rituals you do for your dead before moving the ship. I did say prayers for them, but that is all."

"We say the equivalent of a prayer. I would like to do that if it's all right."

"It absolutely is. I'll feed you afterwards, then you can observe the engine being brought back online and the tow process."

"Thank you. You're kind."

I supposed I was. Other captains would have put him into isolation as a potential threat. For better or worse, I believed his story about the cargo and trusted in his general reaction to seeing a core shiftgem.

Once I delivered him to his world along with his legal cargo, I would do him one more favor: I would identify where the hell those core shiftgems had come from, who in his crew had betrayed him, and why he'd been put into stasis.

The black market held many secrets, and with the right questions, enough money, and some well-placed threats regarding where they got the gems, I might get the answers I needed. In exchange, I would need to get my hands dirty, but it would be worth my while.

Dead men couldn't be punished, and I suspected Delta had ended up in stasis to hide the sins of the other men in his crew. Betrayal happened often in the empty reaches of space.

I would not rest easy until I learned the truth and did something about it. And, should I find which planet the core shiftgems had come from, I would return them to their survivors of the dead world—assuming any existed.

Planet busters cared nothing for the lives lost in their quest for wealth.

FIVE

Only larger ships boasted such features

FIVE HOURS after reviving Delta from stasis, I determined he had escaped without issue. After showing him the process of restoring his ship to life and feeding him, I put him to bed and towed the freighter to the shiftgem gate. While I had needed to change some settings on the freighter, requiring a brief journey to the ship, I'd gotten its engine started and capped it at low throttle, just enough I could dock and tow it along without risk to my engine.

Linking the ships together tested my patience, but four hours after putting Delta to bed, I had both responding to my navigational commands simultaneously. I would hold my breath when it came time to use the shiftgem gate, but I expected we'd make it through without incident.

With the awareness of the cargo I carried, living and dead plus legal and illegal, looming over me, I monitored the space around me, tension cramping my muscles from the general expectation of pirates waiting to ambush me. If word spread from the black market that the ship had an illegal shipment of core shiftgem crystals, they'd chase me across the known universe to get their hands on it.

Once I started poking around to figure out who had acquired it and why, I'd also become a target. However, the knowledge that three men were dead, likely to hide the core shiftgems or transfer blame to Delta, ensured I would do what I could to learn the truth.

Twelve hours after beginning the journey, I reached the shiftgem gate, relieved to be the only vessel present.

The gate itself, an archway embedded with countless glowing shiftgem crystals, offered a light in the darkness, a hope for travelers wanting to find their way home. One moment, the gate would glow white before transitioning to blue then green and every other color imaginable. The first time I'd seen the shiftgem gate, I'd understood how the crystals had gotten their common name.

Scientists called it evolvulite, as the crystal could change its shape and composition in the right conditions, evolving into something else. In the hands of a psionic or psychic, those who defied science with their power of the mind or their ability to reshape reality, the gems could become anything. Some could transform them into metals. Others could reduce them to chip components capable of operating computers.

On Earth, they'd called the compound silica—quartz when it came in one of its crystalline structures.

The inhabitants of Earth hadn't discovered silica's true potential. No, they hadn't even realized their home held lethal secrets, which had ended life on the planet. The cores of shiftgem planets renewed themselves, destroying all life on the surface while redistributing its silica and other precious minerals. Like many planets of its type, volcanoes delivered the payload.

Unlike many other planets of its type, the ocean had played its part as well, evaporating and covering the planet in thick clouds while undergoing its latest evolution. One day, the clouds would fade, the oceans would cool, and life would emerge once more from the planet's shattered ruins.

When it did, *homo sapiens* from the known universe would converge, accept a simpler life, and begin the cycle anew while everyone else stayed away and safeguarded the planet's treasures and life.

I loved the stars too much to be one of those who would let go of everything I'd known to explore a world being reborn in the wake of disaster.

With a renewed quarantine period ahead thanks to my trip to Delta's vessel to get the engines working right, I'd have plenty of time to think about the mysteries of the universe later—after I got us to Cremora Delta's spaceport. The typical anxiety of making a jump settled in, and I brought up my checklist.

Checklists made spaceships fly safely, and the last thing I wanted was to end our lives with a crunch or bang—not that the vacuum of space allowed for the gut-wrenching sound of a crunch or bang.

Once I activated the drive cores, three fates awaited us. The engines would work as normal, the shiftgem gate would act like a doorway, and we'd cross the threshold and emerge on the other side alive, well, and slightly nauseated, the most common symptom *homo sapiens* and similar species endured after passage. If the engines failed to work, we'd float through the gateway without reaching our intended destination.

The final option worried everyone. Failed jumps typically involved spaceships being ripped into pieces, exposing those within to the lethal rigors of space. Some ships were segmented in case of jump failures, designed to create life-saving capsules.

Only larger ships boasted such features.

Sometimes, I dreamed about running one of the larger ships, but then I realized I would need more crew. Life with just Pandora appealed, with brief interludes where I met with other people and told tales of the sketchier adventures out among the stars. Before beginning the process of utilizing the shiftgem gate, I made use of my security system and checked in on Delta to discover my fox had decided to use his feet as her bed. The man still slept, which worked well for me. If something *did* go wrong, he wouldn't feel a thing. If everything went right, he'd get a rude awakening along with my canine companion.

They'd forgive me eventually.

Drawing a deep breath, I held it and began phase one of initiating a jump. I activated my communication system, matched the frequency to the shiftgem gate, and sent a ping to warn other ships someone was about to make the journey across space in the blink of an eye. I initiated a two-minute countdown warning, issued in a series of pings, which would give other ships plenty of time to move out of the landing zone.

My system detected no attempts to communicate or warning pings, which either meant the space on the other end of the gate was empty, my signals were being ignored, or everyone had gotten out of the way.

At the one minute mark, I initiated the shiftgem engines. My ship vibrated as the crystals thrummed to life. I doubted

I'd ever understand how science worked with a splash of the unexplainable, and for the most part, I'd given up trying. The sense of wonder remained. The gate began shifting colors to match the tri-colored cores in both engines, an excellent sign we might make it through in one piece.

At the ten second mark, I exhaled, engaged both engines, and committed to the jump.

Some captains preferred to hit the gate zone at top speed, but I opted for an increasing momentum, allowing the ships to accelerate as they exited the gate on the other side. Once over, I'd kill the engines and allow the vessels to drift while I began system checks to make sure nothing had been damaged during the jump.

The ships hit fifty percent throttle when the nose of the freighter hit the boundary. The stomach-churning lurch of entering the shiftgem gate struck hard, and in the time it took me to yelp and spew a few curses, we were through.

While everyone had cleared the exit point, I had a rather large audience of escort and weapon ships on the other side, and some of the bastards had blocked the deceleration zone. Spitting more curses, I ditched my initial plan of checking the engines, slammed my hand on the warning comm to not-so-politely tell the fuckers to get the hell out of the jump gate exit zone, and reverse throttled both engines, careful to account for the freighter's larger mass.

In good news, the idiot in the deceleration lane understood one of the three curse-ladened languages and got the hell out of the way, although I'd managed to bring my ship and the freighter to a halt before any potential collisions. I deactivated the emergency comm and kept grumbling curses, reset the engines to neutral, and began the checklists for both ships.

I had several warnings from the freighter, but I determined they were from shifted cargo and would be an easy fix for somebody else.

A communication request pinged, and reining in my cussing, I flipped the switch and read off my ship's identification code. The identification response informed me I'd been surrounded by a ridiculous number of Cremoran ships on behalf of Cremora Delta 005-26.

As I wasn't about to let the idiot who'd almost triggered a collision off the hook, once introductions were complete, I said, "Please refresh your assembly regarding the deceleration lane, especially if you're expecting a damaged freighter. Shiftgem gate jumps have a variable speed transition of up to twenty-five percent over ship-base maximum speeds. Collisions at such speeds are not easy to avoid."

"Roger," the man on the other end replied. "What is your current casualty count?"

I accepted the confirmation at face value, reached over, and checked the security cameras to discover a rather annoyed Delta trying to get dressed while Pandora squeaked and did her best to convince him to play with her. Muting the comm system, I activated the intercom and said, "Take your time, Delta. We have successfully navigated the shiftgem gate, and we have been met by a Cremoran fleet for escort. Raise your hand if you can handle playing with Pandora on your own for a while."

His expression changed to amused, and he raised his hand and waved. Then, abandoning the hassle of dealing with the jumpsuit, settled into pet and play with my fox. I flipped off the security cameras, cut off the intercom, and reactivated the ship to ship comm. "There are three bodies in stasis on the freighter and no casualties on board my vessel. Our ten day quarantine period, unfortunately, was reset to starting prior to our jump, as I had to transfer to the freighter to perform some engine repairs. If you were waiting longer than expected, my apologies. The engine was not capable of jumping prior to the fixes I needed to make. The reverse thrust has shifted cargo on board the freighter, but everything was packed fine and shouldn't have been damaged. We just cannot do any tricky flying until the cargo is secured."

"Excellent. And your patient's state following revival?"

"He emerged from stasis with minimal side-effects, although he has been in recovery. His digestive system is fully functional, although he was fatigued prior to entry into stasis. These issues should be resolved by the time we reach the spaceport. Both ships will require quarantining for the minimal ten day period."

"We have prepared a quarantine bay for you, so you will be able to be off ship during the quarantine process. We also have an evaluation clinic in the spaceport in case of illness. Was there any evidence of illness when you boarded the vessel?"

"I simply don't know. The evidence shows asphyxiation due to a failed life support system, but there is no way to know if there were any diseases prior. Cleanup will be minimal. The crew, may they rest in peace, opted to face their deaths in their suits. They were aware they had run out of time and options. According to my patient, they had drawn lots to determine who would be put into stasis."

"Can your ship receive visual data?"

I reached over and activated the display. "Affirmative."

"Can you identify your patient from one of these images?"

Sure enough, Delta's picture appeared along with the images of three other men. None were named, but Delta had been assigned number three. "Number three is the gentleman I revived from stasis. I've dubbed him Delta, as I don't name my cargo, which he doesn't mind. He'll have to remain in quarantine for the whole period, as I will not violate my licensing for captaining my ship. His health is stable, and he did not suffer any impairments as a result of going into stasis. There was one minor complication, likely due to inexperience on the crew's part. He was dosed with a rather high amount of the stasis sedative, but I was able to reverse his sedation without issue. It was a borderline high dosage."

"Thank you for identifying the survivor," my Cremoran contact replied. "What is your xenodiversity rating?"

I rolled my eyes at the question. "If you put me in the same room with a Veloc, sir, I will be inclined to ask if I can touch. I am rated as diverse and minimally xenophobic. If a Veloc opens its mouth in front of me and hisses, I may end up halfway across the galaxy before my flight instinct turns off. I have a high tolerance to non *homo sapiens* species. I have not spent much time with Cremorans, but I have no issues with various tentacles as long as those tentacles do not touch me in inappropriate fashions."

Some women appreciated Cremorans, the lack of pregnancy risk, and their tentacles, which they had in addition to fingers, arms, and their legs.

The Cremoran chuckled. "Excellent. Delta, as you call him, is descended from a line including Veloc, and one of his kin is on board. A cousin. The families branched fairly far back, but their associated generations still consider each other cousins. Bluntly spoken, the Veloc in question is happy to join you for quarantine, but he is very concerned regarding his cousin."

My eyes widened. "I have a *vulpes vulpes* on board."

"A red fox. We were shown pictures of the fox with her rather charming suit. Mystoran, the Veloc, will be careful to befriend your *vulpes vulpes,* so please do not worry. He brings a gift of live prey for your companion, and he will go on a hunt to teach her if she is unaccustomed to live prey."

I pricked my ears forward at that. "She's hunted mice and rabbit before, but it's not something we can do often."

"We shall make certain your companion is entertained for the duration of your quarantine period. How long will it be to get your ships operational? We noticed you had entered neutral for an engine check."

"It's protocol for an engine fresh out of repairs," I assured him. "If you have a proper tug, the engines don't even need to be functional beyond idle thrust, which is in working order."

"We brought a tug with us."

"Be gentle with the docking, as your cargo is loose in the bay. A lot of the shiftgem systems were damaged, and the tethers were non-operational when I boarded the ship. As the shiftgems are well-packed, this isn't an issue, but the system is throwing warnings, and the engines will not go above minimal thrust until those warnings are addressed. I will begin the process of disengaging from the freighter."

"Thank you, sir," he replied.

"Viva, please. Captain Viva if you enjoy being formal."

"I am Pollwin as said by most *homo sapiens.*"

Considering Cremorans had tentacles just about everywhere, including their mouths, his name likely involved squishes, whistles, and trumpets, something my species couldn't readily duplicate. However, I'd learned that most species appreciated effort. "I would be honored with the teaching of your proper name."

Pollwin chuckled. "You must have scored exceptionally well during your xenodiversity licensing."

"The squishes are hard to duplicate, but I've mastered quite a few Veloc trills, some of the hoots, and I can even do a reasonable throat-grumble. As long as you don't do the low-tone thrum as part of your name, I can improvise."

Pollwin made a short trill followed with three short hoots and an amusing squish, one a human tongue *could* replicate. I giggled, and as I had bothered to learn some of the basic greetings in other languages, I greeted him in his tongue with his name.

"That goes far beyond improvisation, Captain Viva. Well learned, well done. How much Veloci do you speak?"

"Enough for conversation, although I am book taught; chances to speak directly to a Veloc are few and far between. I'm a generational *homo sapiens*, so the instructors tried to keep a certain amount of separation. This annoyed me, so I opted to take extended xenodiversity courses. I travel. That means I will meet other species."

"And you're considered unusual for *homo sapiens*, so you are a target for trafficking systems. Having a good xenodiversity rating protects you."

That it did. "It helps when you have extra registrations. So far, my registrations and licensing have done a tolerable job of keeping trouble at bay."

"Before we begin towing, can you inform us on the condition of the cargo?"

"I rummaged through the cargo in search of appropriate crystals and parts to repair the engine, so it's a mess. I have no way of knowing if anything is amiss. There is also no way of knowing if anything was tampered with after the various systems went down."

"Corruption is always a possibility, and knowing which member of the crew went into stasis is very helpful. Once the ship has been fumigated and quarantined, we will do an investigation."

"I will begin the detachment process now, and I will move my ship clear of the freighter's space. I have a link and can operate the ship's engines remotely. Any linker can handle the work, although I'm familiar with the drive's current setup. I had to change crystal colors to bring the ship back into an operational state. Do impress upon the Cremora Deltans that brown shiftgem drives are not suitable for space travel of this nature. I recommend you use the crystal set I installed in a better engine or do a parts change to better work with the new set."

Pollwin hooted a laugh. "Spoken like a true traveler of the stars. I will make certain they are aware that your opinions are sound and should be listened to with upmost respect. It takes quite some skill to replace the colors of the drive. What color did you install in the freighter?"

"Tri-color," I admitted. "It was the most versatile of the shiftgem crystals available compatible with the gate."

"And your engine's core?"

"I also use tri-color for the same reason, although affordability was a factor. Tri-color has more versatility than even blacks, and I haven't met a shiftgem gate I haven't been able to handle yet. I would use a rainbow black set if I could get my hands on one, but the waitlist is as long as the price is high."

"It takes a skilled captain to make use of a rainbow black set."

That it did, as the gems were innately flawed and the prismatic nature of the stones meant versatility *and* volatility. "I've been flying solo for a while now. And I keep a spare set of low-grade crystals on board in case of trouble." Every smart captain did. "Do your ships come with test engines for training purposes?"

"We have training simulators and test sets. Why?"

"My patient would like to learn how to work with crystal installations, and while I taught him the basics on my equipment, I have the feeling he would like the training to be able to prevent another disaster in the future. If you don't cut the quarantine period short, I'm capable of teaching him enough to restore life support and comm systems at a minimum on the basic types. It will not erase the trauma he's endured, but it will do a great deal of good at preventing certain symptoms from manifesting."

For a long moment, Pollwin remained silent. His sigh emerged as a low, almost mournful whistle. "I will make arrangements during the transit to our spaceport. It is only a few hours from here at moderate speed, which we can handle towing with ease. What is the speed capacity of your craft?"

"She's a decent little racer," I announced with pride in my voice. "I haven't actually tested her maximum, but I'm sure I can keep up with your escort with no issues."

"Please detach and stay nearby. We will arrange an escort specifically for your craft unless you would prefer to be towed to spare your engine?"

"My engine is in good condition, and I'll take advantage of the quarantine period to do a full evaluation of her parts.

I'll teach Delta how to handle ship repairs at the same time. He's interested, although I suspect part of that interest is a trauma response."

"He'll undergo appropriate therapy," Pollwin promised. "I will make sure his family is aware of his interest and the potential for trauma. Do you have any allergies?"

"No, I don't."

"Excellent. The spaceport has an excellent quarantining system, so you will be able to enjoy fresh meals without having to use your galley or prefab meals. Your transit history shows very limited stays in ports or on planets. Is there a reason why?"

"Why walk when I can fly?" I replied with a smile.

"I understand that. Disengage from the freighter, and I will have your escort come into position and send you the coordinates for our flight path."

"Roger." I broke off the communication and went to work undocking from the freighter, giving the ship and its sad cargo a salute before easing my ship away to rendezvous with my assigned escort.

Soon enough, the whole business would be behind me, and I would be able to look towards the future—and dig into who had smuggled core shiftgems on the ship and why.

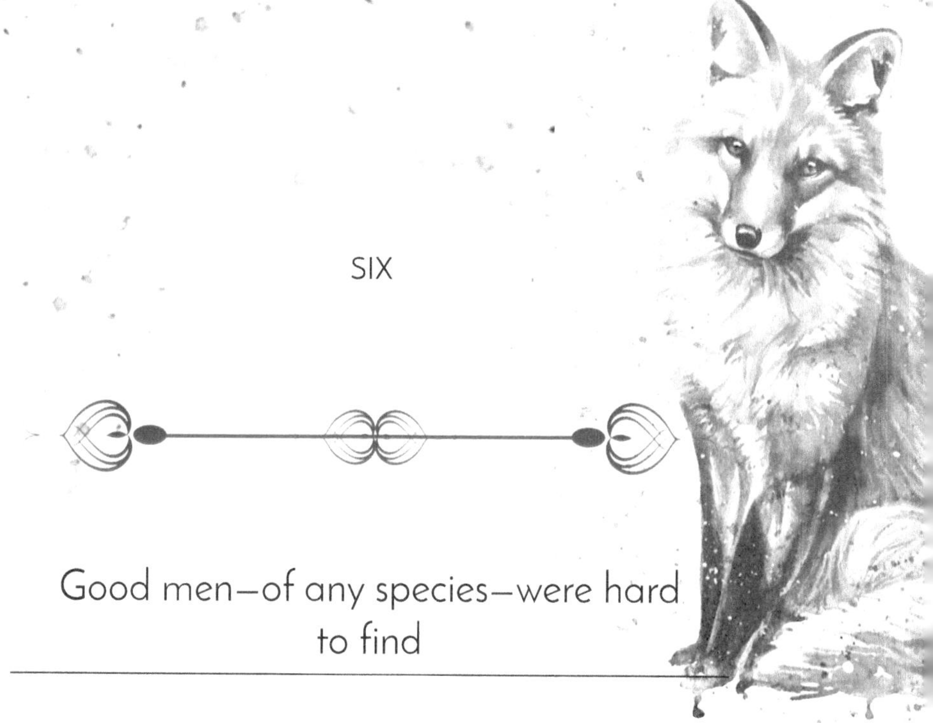

SIX

Good men—of any species—were hard to find

DELTA TOOK my invitation to play with Pandora seriously, and the pair romped until it was time to dock at the spaceport. The man exhausted himself to the point I needed to escort him back to bed, and my traitor of a fox wanted to snuggle with her new pet human. Once the quarantine period ended, I'd have to console her.

Hell, I'd have to console myself, too.

Good men—of any species—were hard to find.

However much he made excellent company and loved animals, we'd have to move on. He had a family to return to, and we had more stars to explore and other unfortunate souls to rescue. Getting attached would do neither of us any good.

Despite knowing that, I hesitated to interrupt Pandora's fun.

She loved people of all shapes and sizes, and I didn't want to destroy that.

Bracing for the inevitable heartache to come within the

next ten days, I took my station in my chair. I followed my escort ship, which would guide me directly to the quarantine bay we'd get to use. The freighter would be taken to the neighboring bay. Corpses and an empty ship took less time to decontaminate. They could use the harsh chemicals with no fear of issues. Living, breathing people needed to use the slower methods, and if one of us became ill, we'd go into isolation in the med bay until we recovered.

Delta would have to cope with learning how to fix engines on the overhaul I'd do on mine and the test engines the Cremorans provided.

At the quarantine bay, I activated my communication system, identified my ship, listed all living passengers, registered I was not carrying any commercial cargo, hadn't been on an active job, and went through the twenty-minute process of registering myself for the spaceport. They informed me my patient was already registered, and that they would issue a collar and tags for Pandora, customized with her name, her species, my name, her authorization code for being in the spaceport, a no-leash authorization, and a little bell. While I questioned the presence of the bell, I acknowledged she needed to wear it while in the spaceport. While they offered no-leash permissions, I'd still leash her in unfamiliar territory, assuming we left the quarantine bay.

An excited fox caused trouble at her whim, and an entire spaceport was nothing but temptation for her.

Before I fled back to the questionable safety of space, I'd do some serious damage to my accounts, spending tokens in one of the few places luxuries could be found off a planet. I expected a haul of digital reading material, educational modules, and a cache of replacement parts.

By the time I finished overhauling my engine and checking for anything that might put me in the same shoes as Delta's deceased crew, I would be limping from paycheck to paycheck.

Well, I might dodge limping from paycheck to paycheck depending on what compensation Delta Cremora 005-26 offered as recovery compensation. Considering the value of the cargo, I expected they would give me enough to make it for a while before I needed to take some necessary risks for my next influx of tokens.

Once approved to enter the bay, I landed my ship on the platform, shut the engine down, and waited for the bay doors to close. I activated the external atmospheric sensors and gravity monitors. Gravity kicked in first, and I shut down my ship's gravity system to give us a chance to adjust to their settings. According to my console, they kept gravity on the lighter side, which would result in a bouncier step than I preferred, although it wouldn't require magnets to get around. Ten minutes after landing, the ship's sensors registered safe levels for *homo sapiens*, and I began the process of equalizing the pressure between the ship and the quarantine bay.

While the systems worked, I pressed the intercom button and said, "We've landed, and equalization should be completed within ten minutes. As we're in quarantine, we'll be permitted to be in the bay but nowhere else until we pass our health checks. Anyone coming into the bay will need to be wearing a hazmat suit or be staying for the entirety of the quarantine period. Expect ten days starting now. We're apparently receiving a Veloc guest to keep us company. I'll be over in a few minutes. I will be leaving the life support system on my ship operational in case of a breach in the bay."

While rare, breaches could happen, and a smart captain maintained a safe haven even when in port. I released the intercom's button and went through my post landing checklist, deactivating everything but the lighting, security, and life support systems.

Once everything checked out, I headed to where I'd left Delta and Pandora. My fox engaged with the man in a vicious game of tug of war with one of her favorite rope toys. Judging from its frayed state, I'd be making her a new one while in the spaceport. "We can disembark now. It seems the Veloc is one of your cousins?"

Delta grinned. "Way back when, one of my great-great-great aunts, with a few extra greats attached, fell in love with a Veloc. When a *homo sapiens* of any sort mates with a Veloc, the result is almost always a Veloc. Their genetics tend to override the genetics of other contributing species. And they have an adaptable reproductive system. The males can reproduce with almost anything. The females aren't quite as adaptable, but *homo sapiens* are genetically compatible with Veloc of either gender. Why? Who knows. But they are, and that's all the Veloc care about. In Veloc society, the *homo sapiens* branch of the family is kept close. So, I have a lot of Veloc cousins as a result, despite the number of generations separating my ancestral aunt having wed a Veloc."

"I was asked about my xenodiversity rating, probably because of your cousin. I only have one rule when it comes to big things with teeth—eat something other than me. I'm not on the menu."

That got Delta laughing. "My family introduces us to our Veloc kin fairly young. It prevents the running and the screaming part of things. Veloc toddlers are soft, fluffy, and have their claws capped. They have teeth, but they're taught not to bite before being introduced to other races. They're more likely to nuzzle you into submission as a result."

Soft and fluffy sounded fun, especially as a child. "I probably insulted them by stating Pandora is not a snack for a Veloc."

"Probably not. It depends on who you were speaking to."

"A Cremoran."

"Then definitely not. They have turned asking Veloc not to eat their family and pets into an art."

"One day, I will find out how us *homo sapiens* lost out on the name game. Everyone else gets dignified species names. Us? Not so much."

"Ah, that's easy enough to explain. Several hundred years ago, humanity opted against being dubbed Earthlings or some other variant of naming with Earth in it. As such, we go by our species designation rather than our home world. So Cremorans and Veloc—and all associated names of races—are proper names and not just a generic species name. I'm of the opinion humanity enjoys making things more difficult than necessary."

That I could agree with. "Are your people Deltans then?"

"We're called that sometimes, yes. If formal, we're Cremora Deltans, which distinguishes us as the adoptees of the Cremorans without being Cremorans."

Damn. "Do the Andromeda *homo sapiens* have something like that yet?"

"Not yet. There are a few species currently bickering to get to claim the planet. Your people will eventually be adopted like mine were. And if you end up picking a different planet, you'll get to claim their name, too."

"It's times like this I have some regrets about skipping straight to space before learning more about what would be waiting for me in space," I confessed, and I gestured in the direction of the cargo bay. Since I was in quarantine anyway, I'd take the time to sort everything, resupply, and prepare for my next adventure. "Pandora, heel."

My fox yipped and heeled as ordered, wiggling her butt in general excitement. I giggled at her antics and rewarded her with a petting. "Once we go greet the Veloc, I'll have treats just for you," I promised. "Play nice with the Veloc. You know those big, mean, nasty predators get sad when they see a fluffy sweetheart like you become afraid. If you're lucky, you'll get more pets."

As Pandora lived for being pet, she whipped her whole hindquarters in her general excitement. I thanked my lucky stars she wasn't one of the *vulpes vulpes* who peed upon reaching maximum excitement capacity. Pandora tended to squeak, and I gave her thirty seconds before she could no longer contain herself.

"I've never wanted an animal more in my life," Delta confessed. "I was concerned about how you handled space alone, but she's smart, she's engaging, and she's soft. I noticed she also enjoys sharing sleeping accommodations with others."

"She's a lot of work, especially when she sheds. I actually keep her fur and sell it to weavers, as it's long, plush, and suitable for spinning. But when she sheds, it's a marvel to behold. I have to be really careful to monitor when she sheds, as it can make a mess of the various systems on board." I headed for the cargo bay, opened the doorway, and sighed at the clutter of lashed down storage boxes, most empty, and the limited remaining supplies waiting for my use. I went to the gangway, pressed the button, and waited for it to lower.

Waiting outside of the danger zone stood a Veloc with cyan blue feathers and a green crest. Perhaps once upon a time, the Veloc could fly, but they'd exchanged wings for lethal, curved claws on their fingers and toes. One such curved claw tapped at the bay floor. Delta grinned, waited for the gangway to lower, and hopped down to greet the Veloc, who towered over him. "Mystoran!"

"Little Cousin," the Veloc replied, lowering his head to brush his muzzle against Delta's cheek. "You had us worried. How do you feel being the potential source of plague, doom, and destruction?"

I chuckled, as I held an equal responsibility in our quarantine situation. I set the ship to lock the gangway into the open position and joined Delta on the ground. I bowed to the Veloc and greeted him in the low trill of his people.

The Veloc's crest snapped open, and he cooed a reply, welcoming me to the spaceport before issuing a series of hoots, trills, and clicks, inquiring on where I'd learned even some of his language.

As I couldn't make the same clicks he could due to the lack of the appropriate tongue and teeth, I improvised with my fingers. Then, aware Delta might not understand Veloc, I translated, "I spend a lot of time alone, so I try to learn other languages so I can navigate dangerous space. I've found most sentients take me more seriously if I can speak a little of their language."

"An accurate translation, and an excellent method of

mimicking our sounds. Well done," Mystoran praised. "You've fallen in with someone unusual, Little Cousin."

"Is his name Little Cousin to you?" I asked, tilting my head to the side.

"It's an honor-title we use for *homo sapiens* of our same generation. I am his elder by a year, so I get to tease him with his age." The Veloc's bright golden eyes, slitted like a cat's focused on Pandora. "And who is this delightful creature?"

With the slow and deliberate care of a predator attempting to mask his nature, the Veloc lowered himself to the floor, resting his claws against the metal to provide the illusion of being less of a threat, bringing his head down to Pandora's level.

I crouched beside Mystoran and patted the floor in front of his muzzle. "Pandora, come meet Mystoran."

Either her excitement of being off ship or my presence beside the Veloc did the trick, but my fox's hold on her general behavior snapped and she yipped and squeaked, wiggled forward, and plowed into the feathered predator, doing her best to snuggle without understanding how to make friends with someone completely covered in down and feathers.

In a way, I envied her and could understand how a human might be enamored with a Veloc.

Mystoran cooed his delight, and when Pandora didn't flinch from him, he splayed his tail, revealing a fortune in glittering jewels hanging from his feathers' shafts. He lifted his clawed hand and pet my fox on the back, careful not to cut her with the sharp tips. I blinked, realizing the tips were covered with caps to blunt them. I peeked at his feet to discover he wore the same caps on his toes as well.

How curious.

"While I'd been informed your new friend was xenodiverse, I had been warned of her pet. It seems the pet is just as xenodiverse as her owner." Mystoran cooed again and nuzzled Pandora. "We will hunt well soon enough, my little friend. Mice and rabbits are plentiful, and we will set up little obstacles throughout the quarantine bay to entertain us while your owner does the busy things captains do when at a spaceport after a long journey."

In Veloc, I informed him I would be most appreciative if he could keep her company, and that the resupply process tested Pandora's patience, which was little on a good day.

He hooted a laugh. "Little Cousin, she has offered her blessing for me to entertain her little fox, so you must keep her company and learn more about space so you do not encounter such trouble in the future."

With a rueful expression, Delta replied, "I've had my fill of such trouble for a few years. That'll be how long it'll take me to have any competence at all."

"Nonsense," I replied, rising to my feet and patting Delta's shoulder. "You'll get the hang of it soon enough. You're ahead of most. You can follow instructions. The hard part will be learning how to read the manual. Once you master that, you'll be all right. Mystoran, what is the process at this spaceport for resupplying post quarantine?"

"You will have docking rights for this bay for the duration of your stay. If you do not want to fuss with going into the spaceport for specific parts and supplies, I can speak with my kin and have the things acquired for you using your token account. A small repayment for bringing him back to us alive and well. It has been at least five generations since anyone in his family line has undergone stasis, and we had no knowledge of his suitability for it."

One day, the truth might bother me less. "It was a last ditch measure on his crew's part. They could try to save one, so they did. Drawn lots, as fair as it gets. They'll likely need me to work on the freighter to explain the adjustments I made, or do additional work on the engine."

"Oh, yes. These bays connect, so you will have full access to the freighter once the bodies are removed. They are doing that now. They will spray the ship down with disinfectant, but it will be safe for humans within three or four hours. I volunteered to help, as engine parts can be heavy and Veloc are strong."

I bet. "I appreciate that. Thank you."

"It is my pleasure. We owe you his life-debt, and that is something we take seriously. You found him in dangerous space, which sees few travelers."

I understood. While it had only taken a few hours to reach the shiftgem gate, luck and luck alone had guided me to Delta and the derelict freighter. Family often appreciated my willingness to scout through space few traveled without good reason.

Once upon a time, the space beyond the shiftgem gate had been bustling, but the spaceport had moved on. People still used the gate to the spaceport's new location, three hops away, but most took a more direct route with fewer jumps.

The shiftgem gate remained, in case someone discovered something more of use or a new spaceport set up operations. I gave it a few years before some enterprising merchant set up another installation, especially if someone wanted to venture off into the uncharted space a few light years away.

Sometimes, I thought about pushing my ship's limits and charting new space. Even a light year worth of additional charting brought in a pretty penny. More died in the attempt than collected pay, although I'd bagged a few tokens from having recovered charting derelicts and their crew.

I'd even gotten credit for the charting, as I'd been the first to reach the uncharted space and return with a map despite the map having been made by someone else.

It helped I'd seen a destination I could verify on their map with only a month's extra travel. I'd one-upped the original mappers, identifying a new planet and its three moons. As was the right of the discoverer, I'd named the planet Pandora-001, and I'd named the moons Vixen, Fox, and Vulpes in honor of my fluffy companion. I wouldn't be the first to take naming things too far. Other planets named Pandora existed, but I'd been the first to use a number to distinguish mine, which meant when the naming authorities swept through the new maps, *my* Pandora would keep its name and the others would be forced to adopt subsequent numbering.

The moons would likewise be protected thanks to my careful numbering of my discovery.

Long after we passed on, my fox would live as a label on a map. She might be more remembered for her crazy owner, but she would be remembered.

Realizing I'd become rather lost in thought, I sighed. "There's no debt owed. Anyone decent in my shoes with my equipment would have done the same. I recover derelicts. That's how I pay for this token guzzler of a ship."

"What is your ship's name?" Delta asked.

"I haven't given her one. I just address her by her identification number in port. Every derelict I've come across were all named. I figure if I break the mold, maybe I won't have that sort of luck. Don't get me wrong. I love my ship, and I worked hard for her—but no names. And not because I don't want to make an attachment, but rather due to the nature of my work."

Mystoran trilled, a sound I interpreted to be amusement. "You have found yourself in company with a most sensible *homo sapiens.* Whatever will you do, Little Cousin?"

"Learn how to fix engines," Delta announced.

I chuckled at his enthusiasm. "Then let's begin. Your first job will be to dismantle my engines and put them back together again. We will evaluate every part, replace those in need of repair, and make certain my ship does not add to the clutter littering space."

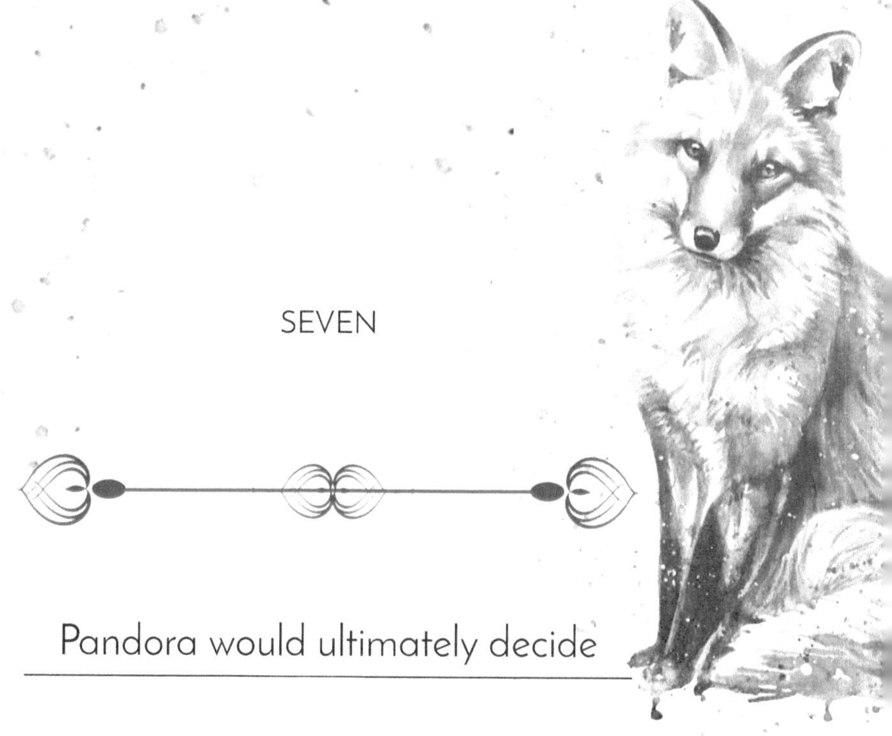

SEVEN

Pandora would ultimately decide

FOR SEVEN DAYS, we overhauled my engines, and I taught Delta the name of every part, the importance of every bolt, and how the shiftgem crystals interacted with everything to create energy capable of hurtling my ship through space. To test his work, I used the comm system to request hover authorization in the quarantine bay, which had plenty of space for the three feet I wanted in every direction to test the system.

They gave me flight authorization for outside of the bay, promised a tug if the engine didn't check out, and recommended I fly around Cremora Delta 005-23, which was a half-hour flight from the spaceport. I accepted the offer with delight, requested thirty minutes for flight preparations, checks of the other systems, and boarding the excitable Veloc and my *vulpes vulpes*, who hunted through a maze of cargo crates together.

I feared I would need to leave my precious fox with her new friend, who handled her energy and quirks with grace.

Pandora would ultimately decide, as the vigor of space often wore the animal down. I did my best, but sometimes, my best wasn't enough—not when the feathered predator might be able to offer my fox a better future.

Rather than worry about it, I whistled for the pair, who came running over, both on all fours, continuing their elaborate game of chase. The Veloc won, although I doubted Pandora understood she'd been beaten by someone many times her size. "Delta's done his first engine overhaul, and the spaceport has granted permission to do a flyby of Cremora Delta 005-23 to do a full system check in a live environment. You can come if you would like."

"I would," Mystoran replied, rising to his feet and scooping up Pandora before she could run off and lose us precious time. "Might I inquire where you received such a fine beast?"

"My parents bred her from their *vulpes vulpes.* I'm sure you could inquire with the Andromeda *homo sapiens* for one. The kits don't go cheaply to outsiders, but I'll vouch for you if you would like a pair of foxes. They usually are sold in unrelated pairs to allow them to breed. There are rules about the kits born, though. They have to be sterilized or sent to unrelated owners in a trade. If you breed, you can inquire with other owners for trading kits to establish a healthy population on your world if they're determined to be a viable introduction to the environment. If not, you'll have to verify the location and state of all *vulpes vulpes* on the planet."

"Tedious but reasonable. I will inquire. She is a remarkable creature. I am amused she often checks on you in the lulls between our hunts and games."

She'd been checking on me? I smiled and rewarded my fox with a petting. "You are such a good girl."

Once I had the gangway closed, I ordered Pandora to go to her bed for launch. The instant Mystoran set her down, the fox ran for her launch station. "She has a special padded nest she hides in for launches. Foxes aren't built well for seat harnesses, and with a fresh engine overhaul, things could get bumpy. Usually, we only do this for planetary launches. Getting a ship of this model in and out of orbit is rough. She's rated for it, but she much prefers spaceport docking." I gestured to the quarantine bay. "This is just luxury."

"Most of the docks here are enclosed with gravity. It's an expensive spaceport, but it is favored by long distance travelers. Your docking fees are covered by the spaceport itself, as its owned and operated by Cremora."

I guided the pair to my main navigation room, grateful I'd opted to have seating enough for five sentients. "I'll apologize in advance for the discomfort, Mystoran. I was informed most Veloc would become quite unreasonable about my ship and would rather risk life and limb in a blackhole than venture out on a death trap like this."

Mystoran hooted his amusement. "My tail shall be fine, no worries. We are masters of lounging in chairs meant for smaller sentients. I would replace a seat were I to fly long term, but that would be my expense rather than yours, for I am vain and my tail is beautiful."

That it was. "I'd say buckle up, but uncap those claws and dig your toes in if something goes wrong. The belts aren't rated for your weight and would rip right out anyway."

The Veloc chuckled, picked one of the seats, and made himself as comfortable as he could.

"I have to do a walk around the ship, which basically involves making sure there's nothing loose that can cause problems, shut all the doors, raise the gangway, and so on. It'll take about ten minutes. Gossip while I'm gone, but don't touch any buttons. You won't get to fly this go around, Delta, but I might let you get a taste for it after quarantine is over and I can submit paperwork for you to do a test flight."

"A generous offer," the Veloc murmured.

"You don't mind?"

"I don't mind at all. Consider it some temptation to get you back into space again. If you can fix it *and* you can fly it, you're a lot safer in the vast unknown. Make your own security." That way, no one would be able to take his peace of mind away from him, even in the middle of a disaster.

He might not get lucky twice, but he wouldn't die with the crushing weight of helplessness closing in.

He would die trying.

"I'd go back. It would be reluctantly, but I'd go back if needed," Delta replied.

I pointed at the co-captain's chair, which was near mine. "You can sit in that chair, and you can watch and learn."

Delta obeyed, and I went on my walk around my ship, fetched a few treats and a new bone for Pandora, and took to her launch nest and gave them to her. I checked the nest's ties, buttoned the entry so she could escape with some work but not as a result of a rough takeoff or landing, and checked over the rest of the ship, which I'd kept flight ready. Satisfied, I closed and locked the gangway, input the security codes into the system to lock the ship down, and returned to my seat. Pleased, I buckled in, coached Delta on how to secure his belt, and began my checklists for launch.

I opened the comm link, identified my ship, and requested flight authorization from the quarantine bay to do a complete system check, establishing my planned route to Cremora Delta 005-23 and back to the same bay. The traffic controller approved, notified me I would be performing a gravity based takeoff, and began the process of preparing the quarantine bay for access to open space.

"Gravity based takeoff?" Delta asked. "Why is that significant?"

"Essentially, when gravity is on when I take off, I will have takeoff velocity propelling me out of the spaceport. This can result in a rather hasty departure from the spaceport. As we're at a quarantine bay, most ships are on the other side of the spaceport, so we can zip in and out at a much higher velocity. We'll come in at a crawl, and it wouldn't surprise me if the spaceport staff disinfects the quarantine bay while we're gone and leaves supplies—and possibly dinner—as we won't be under foot to infect them."

Mystoran chuckled. "They know we're not infected with anything at this stage. They have viral scanners in the quarantine bay. They're just testing your ethics."

I snorted, as most spaceports pulled that trick at least once or twice in a captain's career. "It was unlikely we were infected, but corpses in space can cause trouble in a hurry. It's better safe than everyone sorry."

"Precisely," the Veloc agreed.

"Captain Viva, you are approved for takeoff at your leisure. Space is clear around your bay. Have a safe flight. We have full comm reach with Cremora Delta 005-23, and there is a tug available should you encounter any system difficulties."

"Roger." I changed the frequency to general spaceport monitoring to listen in on other flights coming in and out in case someone decided to venture off their authorized path while beginning my support system startup. I confirmed the life support system first, nodded at no warnings, and started the engine.

The ship purred with a hint of a thrum, and I smiled at the sound. "And that is what a good engine sounds like. Well done, Delta. Let's see how she handles, shall we?"

The quarantine bay doors opened, revealing empty space and a blanket of stars, and I engaged the hover thrusters. My ship wobbled before stabilizing. One day, I would get around to identifying the source of the wobble and fix it, but as I expected the wobble, and she maintained her position three feet above the bay floor, I considered it to be Delta's victory.

"Hover thrusters are all functioning normally," I announced, before easing the throttle forward. My ship glided towards the bay doors. "Ready to see what tri-color crystals can do?"

"Absolutely," Delta replied.

"You're biting off more than you can chew, Little Cousin," the Veloc warned. To my amusement, the feathered predator braced.

Smart.

I activated both my forward and rear thrusters to maintain position, throttled the engine to seventy-five percent power, and with a wicked grin, killed the forward thrusters. With a thrum I felt more than heard, my ship zipped into space, left the spaceport's gravity, and bolted in the general direction of Cremora Delta 005-23. Using my link, I brought up the space chart for the area, established the correct trajectory to slingshot around the planet, and increased throttle to ninety percent.

At long last, due to persistence, new parts, and careful calibration, I'd gotten my baby to hit close to max engine capacity without a bone-rattling vibration. Delta would carry some of the credit, although I'd gone over every piece of his work, checked it to my satisfaction, and if it hadn't been to my satisfaction, I'd made him dismantle the part in question and start over until he did it right.

In the seven days the project had taken, I'd come to appreciate his patience, his attention to detail, his willingness to learn, and his somewhat twisted sense of humor, especially when we'd gotten a face full of oil thanks to one of his errors.

It had taken him three hours to clean up that mess to my satisfaction, and I'd laughed the entire time.

I hadn't been much different the first time I'd taken oil to the face.

Once I confirmed the engine wouldn't break apart on me near max capacity, I lowered the throttle and eased the ship to a saner traveling speed. In my co-captain's seat, Delta clutched the armrests. Mystoran had restrained himself, thus leaving my ship without any new holes, but his feathers stood on end.

"Problem?" I asked, careful to keep my amusement out of my voice.

"I don't think that was legal," the Veloc whispered.

"It was legal. The traffic controller knew I wanted to do a full engine test, which is why she cleared space near the quarantine bay and had a tug nearby. If there was something wrong with the engine, I would have stalled leaving the bay and would have needed the tug. By testing the hover and throttle, I gave the engine a workout in a safe environment. Shiftgem drives don't typically explode—not in the way a combustion engine does. As such, the only thing to be damaged would be my engine room if something went wrong. Seventy-five percent thrust *is* the maximum I can depart a spaceport in this specific ship."

"Are you sure it was legal?" the predator asked in a wavering tone.

I giggled and nodded my head. "Had it not been legal, you would have heard the traffic controller verbally tear me to pieces for the entire spaceport to hear. You all right, Delta?"

"Do I have to be insane to pilot a spaceship?"

"Not insane, but a little crazy helps. That was a fairly standard maneuver. You need to master it to gain sufficient acceleration to break free of a planet's gravitation pull. Exit velocity varies by planet, and no one planet has the same exact exit velocity. Some planets are harder to escape than others. Spaceports are a good way to learn how to handle controlling a ship when transitioning from gravity to no gravity. Spaceports are different in that they have set zones. The bay had gravity right until the doors, after which there was only the natural gravitational pulls of nearby planets and stars. You'll learn to love and hate gravity." I confirmed my trajectory would send us directly to Cremora Delta 005-23 before unbuckling and relaxing in my seat. Pressing the intercom button, I said, "Pandora, you're free to roam."

"That was *standard*?" Delta blurted.

I laughed. "If you decide you want a piloting license, you'll be pulling a lot nicer stunts than that one. I was just stress testing the engine in a safe place. If that test had failed, the tug would have retrieved us, pushed us back in the bay after they cut gravity, put us in position, and restored gravity, where I'd be spending the next few weeks repairing her to be flightworthy. That was a successful stress test. I wouldn't be surprised if the traffic controller assigned us an escort to make sure we didn't have engine troubles since they're aware I just did an overhaul with a baby mechanic. That's you."

"Well, you proved I knew nothing, but now all I have rattling around in my head are part names, bolt sizes, and a memory of what oil tastes like. I'm making it my mission to never taste that again."

"That's a good goal to have. It only takes once. So, piloting for beginners." I pointed at the star chart I'd brought up, giving me a view of the space in front of the ship. "Ships come with autopilot, so I set a trajectory using that. The ship then changes directions unless I'm manually piloting. Right now, I'm running the autopilot, as I want to make certain all my systems are working properly." I directed my finger out the front window. "Space is full of debris. This section will be relatively clean, as they hire ships to destroy space trash and monitor for rocks and so on. But debris can happen at any time." I pressed a button to bring up the information panel on my ship's weaponry. I gestured to the activated weaponry system. "That is our first and last defense against small space debris. If it's too small to vaporize, I dodge it, which is when I override autopilot. My detection systems can pick up space debris two minutes out if it's a dangerous size, which will trigger various alarms. Autopilot is smart enough to dodge—usually. But if an alarm goes off, I take over and make certain we avoid a collision. For me, usually isn't good enough, and I stopped counting the number of derelicts I've salvaged because they gambled on the usually and lost."

"And my ship?" Delta asked, his tone quiet.

"Bad luck. Just infernally bad luck." And someone with something to hide and the realization there was no other way out. For all I knew, it could have been a situation where they'd intended the ship to be picked up by someone else and the cargo stolen, with Delta as an additional prize.

Until I hit up one of the black markets, I wouldn't know, not for certain. But soon enough, I'd go to the distant parts of space where the smart survived, the cunning cheated everyone else of their hard-earned tokens, and I might be able to review the black market logs through calling in a favor from an operator I'd bailed out from trouble in the deepest reaches of space.

What I learned would dictate my future choices.

I pushed the thought aside and began the tedious process of teaching Delta how my ship worked, how to control her, and gave him a taste of what it meant to be wild and free, slingshotting the vessel around the desert world of Cremora Delta 005-23 and back to the spaceport.

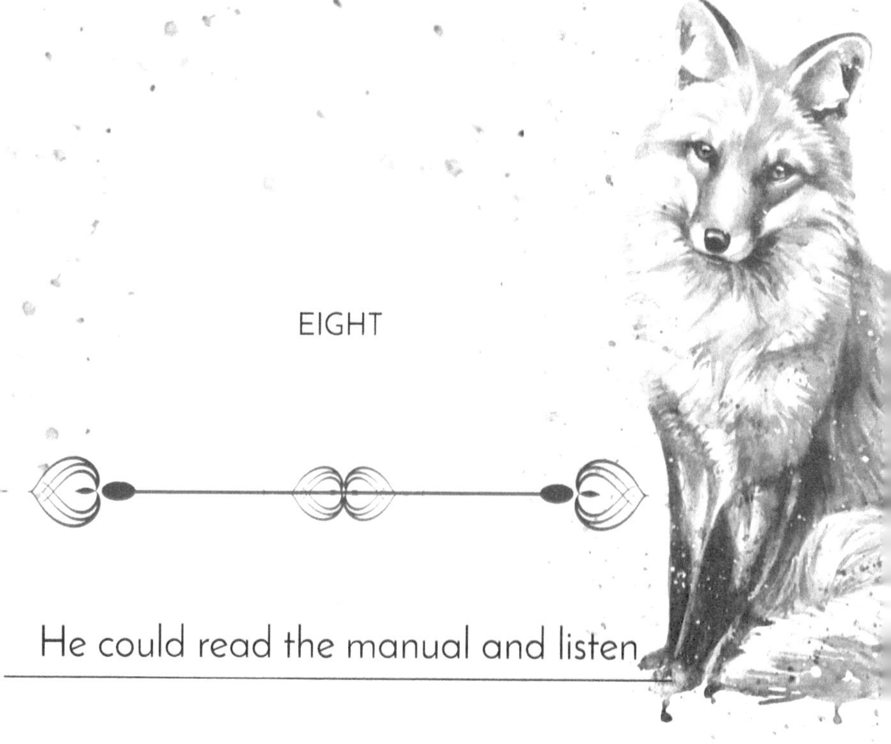

EIGHT

He could read the manual and listen

AS PROMISED, I filed an application for Delta to have a legal lesson in captaining my ship. The spaceport authorized a three-hour cruise. The flight path amused me, as it would take us on a tour around the spaceport. Traffic control asked me nicely to avoid slingshotting around Cremora Delta 005-23, as there would be other ships in orbit who would appreciate not having heart attacks.

I laughed and confirmed I would not have a beginner attempt to slingshot any planet, star, or other stellar object.

To my delight, the spaceport authorized him flying my ship out of the quarantine bay, something most disallowed due to the higher risk of a novice pilot making a critical error. Delta sat in my seat, and the poor man sweat.

Mystoran did a better job of hiding his discomfort, but the Veloc's crest lay flat to his skull, and he clutched the armrest with his capped claws.

As I intended to make Delta take it slow and easy, I allowed Pandora to sit in the co-captain's chair in her harness, which was clipped to the seat. I petted my fox, pleased she'd slept with me the entire quarantine period rather than snuggling up with her feathery friend.

Once we returned from his maiden flight, Delta would leave quarantine and go home with Mystoran, and I would resupply my ship with some help from Mystoran's kin. Within five hours of our return, I would be on my way to the black market to find out the truth of the core shiftgem crystals hiding beneath my engine.

"All right, Delta." I pointed at the comm button. "Press that button and tell the traffic controller my ship identification number, your status as a temporarily licensed training captain, and that you wish to depart from our quarantine bay to head to the first set of coordinates on our flight path." I took the time to tell him precisely how to phrase the entire thing and had him repeat it back to me before setting him loose.

He did as told, and the traffic controller approved our departure, informing us he would have all space cleared for an additional ten minutes to account for novice piloting education.

At my prompting, Delta confirmed reception of the transmission.

"All right. We're not going to do a stress test of the engine, but I'm going to teach you how to do the same maneuver but at a lower speed." I reached over, pressed the communication button, and said, "Instructor Captain Viva here; we will be practicing the orbital escape launch at a quarter speed. Approval requested."

"Approval granted up to thirty percent speed," the traffic controller replied.

"Roger." I directed Delta on how to change to the

correct frequency for the next stage of launch. "Checklists are a way of life, but as you are not a linker, you can't make use of my specific checklists, so I will relay the checklist to you. Do as you're told, and you'll learn."

"Roger," he said, and he swallowed.

Step by step, I coached him through the basic system checks, which took a little longer than my normal, but he managed with admirable speed for someone handling the complicated instructions for the first time. Once he made it through the safety checklists, I had him start the engine.

As everything felt and sounded normal, I directed him on the first phase of launch, which involved hovering the ship three feet over the quarantine bay floor and directing the ship's flight path to the correct angle to safely leave the spaceport. The quarantine bay doors opened. A single tug waited off to the side, a protocol that would be present until my departure.

They took engine overhauls seriously, and a quick tug could prevent disaster—and bring us safely to a halt if the engine failed partway through leaving the area.

"Initiate forward and rear thrusters to twenty-five percent," I instructed, gesturing to the correct controls on the seat. He obeyed, and he took care to initiate thrust at the same rate. Given time and good coaching, I suspected he'd make a damned good captain.

He could read the manual *and* listen.

I'd miss having intelligent company capable of speaking the same language when I ventured to the black market.

Once he had my ship purring and ready to go, I said, "Forward thrusters to zero percent."

Without the forward thrusters holding the ship back, she zipped out of the quarantine bay and hit the vacuum of space at the appropriate speed. "Maintain speed," I ordered, and informed him how to lock the thrusters into position. Then I guided him through establishing a flight path to our first set of coordinates before having him send a communication to the control tower we had cleared the spaceport and were on route to our destination.

I unclipped Pandora's leash and gave her permission to roam, and to my amusement, she went to the Veloc and began squeaking at him in her version of reassurance.

"I can't tell if she's telling me off or what," Mystoran admitted.

"She's trying to comfort you. She thinks you're scared."

"Oh, I *am* scared. Little Cousin is flying a spaceship, and we haven't died yet."

"We won't be dying today. This is an easy flight. I'll spare your nerves and handle the landing portion, as that requires a license he is not qualified to hold yet. The only reason he got away with an orbital escape launch is because I hold a higher license and am qualified to teach it. It's also fairly basic and easy on this ship and in the conditions at the spaceport, which also help. I have enough hours in space as a captain to hold the top-level license." I took over the co-captain's seat and made myself comfortable. "Now you just get to adjust our flight path as we reach coordinate points and see where the spaceport is sending us out on our cruise. If they're assholes, they'll send us into an asteroid belt."

"There are no asteroid belts close enough to reach in the time we're allowed. Fortunately," the Veloc reported. "But we'll fly by his home world. It's the farthest point in the flight path. I may have requested that on purpose."

I chuckled. "It's pretty close to the spaceport, then."

"There's a shiftgem gate."

Damn it. I laughed at the ruthlessness of the control tower and the spaceport operators. "It's your lucky day, Delta. You get to learn how to jump my ship. Oh, this will be fun."

"Fun for you, maybe," Delta muttered.

I laughed and nodded. "Fun for me. Don't worry. You might have some fun, too. I'll get you back to the spaceport safe and sound."

DELTA HANDLED MOST of the flight, but when we reached his home world, I shooed him out of my seat and had him gawk at his planet. After a brief discussion with one of the planetary traffic controllers, I received authorization to enter the atmosphere for a better tour of the world. The green and blue planet with a smattering of deserts and mountains seemed like the perfect place for humanity to live. I spotted several cities, staying far from their territory and at the appropriate altitude to appease the traffic controllers.

When we flew around a city nestled on a plain a short distance from a mountain and an ocean, Delta pointed at it. "That's where I live."

The place had a fixation on skyscrapers, and I spotted at least one launchpad for spaceships. "Nice place. Prettier mountains." I contacted traffic control and requested permission to reenter space from our coordinates, which was granted. I accelerated, pleased with my engine's purr and light thrum even when I pushed her to ninety-five percent. We broke through the atmosphere into space, and I charted our next coordinate on the flight path and gave the controls back to Delta. "You'll be back home by the end of the day probably, if it's that close. Hell, I could have just tossed you out the back if I'd wanted to deal with imports. I'm impressed they didn't give me more of a fuss about doing a tour."

"You're on the authorized list from the spaceport," Mystoran informed me. "The spaceport would have filed a flight authorization for you to orbit the planet, and it's not unusual for curious tourists to want to enter the atmosphere. As you went through the proper entry protocols and wasn't landing, it was approved. Normally, Cremora Delta 005-26 bars unexpected entries unless in an emergency. The inhabitants of this planet are not as xenodiverse as some might appreciate. They're xenodiverse with Cremorans and Veloc, but other races tend to create issues. You're probably quite the novelty, really."

"Was it the ears or the tail?"

"Both, really. And that they're attached to a *homo sapiens* is even more remarkable."

"Genetic manipulation for survival. Mostly, it makes me exceptionally adorable and difficult to dress." I laughed at my own joke. "There are a few races who see my ears and *lose their shit* over it. I'm the cutest damned thing they've ever seen, and then they see my tail, and I sometimes need to dig out fainting salts to help them get over it."

"I wish I could claim that was an exaggeration, but we Veloc are not immune to the allure of ears and tail. The first time someone modded a human for your adaptations, an entire planet of my kin went mental wanting to romance the entire species. We take our romancing quite seriously."

"What was the planet's success rate on romancing?" I asked, and I didn't bother to hide my amusement.

"Two genetically modified human women opted to move to Veloci Minor. Every now and then, a Veloc will be born with unusual ears or a different style of tail, reminding us we carry diverse genetics. Those Veloc are disgustingly alluring, if I do say so myself. Once one is born, every unrelated clan attempts matchmaking. The scheming starts early, but the young hopefuls don't start competing until they're in their early twenties. That's the equivalent of our late adolescence, when my species becomes quite interested in romancing. The ears and tail are wretchedly alluring."

I chuckled at Mystoran's complaint. "I was designed so the tails and ears would be a dominant trait. They weren't sure how planetary adaption should work out, but my genetics were completely overwritten to be full dominance for my ear and tail characteristics. After a few generations, it might become a recessive trait, but I'm not sure. I was notified the trait was aggressively dominant."

"It is much like Veloc genetics. Aggressive dominance will overwrite the recessive genetic traits of your offspring and ensure the survival trait survives. In humans like yourself, the aggression may degrade after ten or so generations, but were you to wed a Veloc, your children would all have ears and tail, no matter what the remainder of the genetics would be. A desired trait among my people—and most, really. Outside of the necessary care, your hearing is likely exceptional. Do your other ears function?"

"Both sets of ears function," I confirmed. "And yes, I have superior hearing even compared to the *vulpes vulpes* the genetics were derived from."

"Ah, once word spreads, expect to be romanced most

seriously. When I go home and tell my clan about Little Cousin's adventures, you will become a target of Veloc and human alike."

I rolled my eyes over the absurdity of the situation, although a treacherous part of me hoped someone like Delta would be in the hunting party. "Oh, no. I'm being threatened with interstellar romance. Whatever shall I do?"

"Run. It's more fun that way," the Veloc replied.

I LANDED my ship in the quarantine bay, waited for the doors to close and the life support systems to make the space habitable, and escorted my two guests off to the rest of their lives. The grapevine had done its work, and Delta's family had come to meet him. I opted to bypass the tearful family reunion, called for Pandora, and gave her the choice to decide if she wanted to keep Mystoran company while I went back into space or stay with the crazy chick.

She chittered a rebuke at me, and to make it clear she would not be leaving, went into her nest and chittered at me some more. I apologized to her, bribed my way back into her good graces with a fresh bone and some treats, and promised we'd be lifting off within the next four to six hours to go on our next adventure.

I waited for the family gathering to disperse, and they took Delta off for his journey home. The rare happy ending, where someone lost managed to come home, reminded me why I took the risks.

The ship would be quiet for a while, and I'd miss his relentless stream of questions, his determination to learn, and his fledgling desire to see more of the stars. I'd even miss the Veloc, although I doubted I'd ever get used to the vast distance he could pounce upon prey. Pandora would miss a hunting companion, but I'd make sure she would be able to hunt the next time we landed, even if I had to find mice to buy for her.

With the guests gone, I went to work resupplying, checking over the list I'd asked Mystoran's Veloc kin to provide. I'd tried to pay them for everything, but they'd taken the whole life-debt issue seriously, refusing to accept my trade account details.

They *had* accepted the information for my primary token account, which they'd use to send compensation for the recovered cargo. Due to trade and recovery rules, it would be three weeks until the tokens showed up, which would be dispersed into several other currencies associated with my account and a base token supply.

Everywhere accepted tokens, but the value of a token sometimes decreased, so I tried to keep an available stash of the top six currencies used throughout the universe.

It simplified my life.

But in a pinch, I'd have tokens enough to get me through the next while without complication.

I wondered how much the Cremora Deltans thought their cargo was worth. As I hadn't set a rate, compensation ranged from a single token to hundreds of thousands. I'd been on single token jobs before. I'd learned strange things happened in space on that job. Before I'd gotten offended, I'd been smart enough to check my ship over carefully, discovering a fortune of supplies and parts in my cargo bay, all of which had been registered as taxes paid, signed off to me as the sole owner.

They'd loaded my ship while I'd been dealing with other paperwork.

The requested supplies, already loaded into my preferred storage crates, waited at near the doors, and a pair of dark-colored Veloc skulked in the shadows, betrayed by their emerald crests.

Sometime after my heart rate returned to something sane, I said, "You get full points for your camouflage techniques. Did Mystoran sacrifice you to be muscle?"

The shorter of the two lowered his head and bobbed, his crest feathers rising. "We are being taught why to respect our elders. We must help load your ship without damaging anything." He displayed his capped claws. "We have our caps on, and we will be careful."

I realized I dealt with the equivalent of troublesome teens, and I chuckled at the realization I'd been given a pair of baby Veloc to work with. "Come along then, kiddos. Ever been aboard a ship like this before?"

Both of them shook their heads, and their crests napped into upright position, showing off their bright feathers. After watching Mystoran, I'd learned the crest communicated interest and curiosity as much as the Veloc used them to express other emotions.

I assumed I had excitable children to teach, which worked for me.

They weren't much taller than me, and they had a lot of growing left to do, judging from Mystoran.

I showed them how to pick up one of the storage containers without damaging them and brought them on board, checking the digital labels to determine their basic contents and setting them up. "These lock into place using magnets so they won't shift during flight. The type of storage container varies. Some are freezers powered with shiftgem crystals, others are for dry storage, and some are for parts. I blew through a lot of parts doing my engine check," I admitted, gesturing to the empty space I'd once used for my ship supplies. "If we get this loaded up in a hurry, I'll show you the engine room and my revival equipment."

The offering worked, and with the energy only children possessed, the Veloc turned the loading process into a race. They kept score on the number of crates I secured into place, and they only counted the tally when their box was nestled in its proper spot. I appreciated that, and I resisted chuckling while they were present.

In record time, I had everything loaded up, and everything seemed to be present. I had a few new storage containers, all a newer model of the ones I liked, which claimed to contained stasis-frozen fruits, vegetables, and meats. Mystoran must have tattled regarding the capacity of my galley, which went beyond the standard setups for most small ships. I could, when I wanted, actually cook. I could also make use of nutrient cubes, which I could make on the fly with anything edible.

I refused to question the containers of stasis-frozen food, as I would appreciate them given a week. Once finished, I took the Veloc on the promised tour, introduced them to Pandora, and lost thirty minutes letting them play with my fox, careful to make sure nobody got too rough.

I expected their families would be out for my head, and not for romantic purposes, when the kids declared they wanted pet foxes of their own.

At the four and a half hour mark, I did my walk around, put Pandora in her nest with a treat, and prepared to leave the spaceport. I made use of the data link to transmit the inventory the Veloc had put together along with the notifying the spaceport I had not been the one to stock the ship and that the goods had been checked by spaceport authorities prior to being loaded.

If something did happen, I'd be covered.

Ten minutes later, the traffic controller gave me authorization to leave, wished me well on my journey, and briefed me on current space conditions on route to the nearest shiftgem gate.

I couldn't help but wonder what the future would hold—and how far of a head start the Veloc and their romance-crazed kin would give me.

NINE

One of them was the prized rainbow black

THREE DAYS INTO MY JOURNEY, I drifted off course, killed my engine, and accessed the storage spot for the core shiftgems, which had gone without detection in the quarantine bay. I would make use of other nooks and crannies for the crystals, which would be difficult to access without requiring me to tear apart my engine to make it happen. I regretted undoing a lot of Delta's work, erasing all evidence he'd been around and about in the process.

I did a top to bottom search of the cargo container, discovering several more caches of core shiftgems in a range of sizes from twenty centimeters down to half a centimeter. Several had already been turned into necklaces, the chains simplistic and styled to hide the origin of the stone. At first glance, nobody would know the difference between a standard shiftgem and the illegal treasures I'd pilfered.

One of them was the prized rainbow black, and it warmed in my hand as though resonating with my skin. It had been wrapped in silver wire to capture the stone's rich color. At a little over four centimeters long, it fell into the tiny but fierce category.

I slipped it over my head and tucked it beneath my clothes, and if anyone asked, I would claim I'd picked it up as a bauble at some spaceport market. Smaller stones often went up for sale for a pittance, unsuited for more important tasks. Rainbow blacks showed up often enough at standard mines, and few wanted them.

They were too difficult to work with on a good day.

I evaluated each stone with a magnifier and scanner, and while they registered as core shiftgems for crystal type, none of them had been marked with a serial number, confirming they were either stolen from a mine or had come from a planet busting operation.

The mines tended to have excellent security, and few stones emerged without being imbued with their serial number.

Without serial numbers or evidence of psychic imprint, I'd have to venture off to a black market and hit up a contact who'd be happy to pay back a debt he owed me.

While he'd started life as a *homo sapiens*, Carthello had undergone so many genetic modifications he no longer classified as even remotely human. He'd borrowed from the Veloc, boasting a rainbow crest and sharp talons on his fingers. He'd also stolen genetic material from one of the stranger denizens of space, a blend between a giant bird, a lizard, and a cat. He'd gotten a bit of everything with that modification, although his beady, lizard eyes never failed to creep me out—especially as he'd gotten ten of them for reasons I failed to understand. Add in a few tentacles from the Cremorans, and he'd qualify for his own species designation if he ever bothered to fill out the form.

I questioned his tail, which had characteristics of the Cremoran tentacles and a lizard's with a light coating of fur jutting up between the scaled hide. I questioned the scales, as they reminded me of some fish. The presence of gills on his neck implied he *had* acquired aquatic DNA from somewhere.

I'd given up guessing.

To reach the black market, I needed to do a series of fifteen shiftgem jumps, which tested my nerves, my engine, and my shiftgem crystals more than I liked. I stuck to batches of three jumps a day before checking my systems over with a fine-toothed comb and repeating the process. To add to the complexity, I cruised at least a day from the gates in a direction few ventured to make myself less of a target during the journey.

A month and a half after leaving the spaceport, I arrived at my destination, an old, battered station that might have become a spaceport if the operators had opted to keep their hands clean. As no black market op bothered with traffic control, I eased my ship around until I found an available docking station, claimed it as mine, tethered my ship, and got suited up, opting to bring Pandora with me and on a close leash.

She would turn my ship into a target if I left her on board. Then, because I was an asshole, I locked the ship up tight, engaged the warning system that promised sonic hell among other things for those who messed with my ship, and began the tedious journey to the station's interior.

The Veloc had done more than just add new cargo containers to my bay; they'd given me advanced units, the kind I cried over upon their discovery from joy one was finally *mine*.

The case I carried might draw unwanted attention, but then again, any attention in the black market counted as unwanted. The wise would honor the rules.

I wouldn't mess with them, they wouldn't mess with me.

Once inside the station, gravity kicked in, although my suit informed me they no longer had a functional life support system. I chuckled at the signs the market would be moving on. Knowing Carthello, he would be the first to know it was time to leave but the last to actually do so.

I headed for his regular haunts, and the smuggler and operator did not disappoint, slithering in my direction with a new set of snake coils to go along with the rest of his modifications. He flashed a series of numbers at me with his fingers, and I connected to the frequency.

"I'm surprised you're here," Carthello stated, and his voice had picked up a rather bubbly quality since the last time we'd spoken. "News on the wire is hot for you. You have captured the attention of a Veloc clan."

"Emerald Crests?" I replied, chuckling. "I was told to run to make it interesting."

"Ah. You are aware they find you interesting, then?"

"They're no problem. They get along with Pandora, and they're not bad for huge predators. How dare me for impressing their younglings and teaching them the glories of space. I'm a terrible influence. I might run a high risk of being romanced by some Cremora Deltans or their Veloc cousins. I recovered the cousin of a Veloc from a derelict. He survived to tell the tale. I tried to impart I had zero interest in life-debts, but Veloc do not listen when they've decided something, I've noticed. It's no matter. I do have an important matter to discuss in private."

"Follow," he ordered, and he guided me deep into the

belly of the dying beast. "You're lucky. We're leaving in a month. I'll give you the coordinates for the new spaceport. We're trying something new."

I laughed at the whole idea of black market ops trying something they considered to be new. "What, you're going legal?"

"In part."

Nice. "You can sign me up for your legal operations—for a price."

"That is actually why I'm rather glad you made an appearance. I *would* like you for our legal operations. You've the cleanest record we've seen."

"Not so clean right now."

"Ah. Trouble?"

"In plenty. It's not something *I* did, but I would like to clear a Cremora Deltan of a crime his crew likely did."

"What kind of crime?"

"In private."

He waved a few tentacles, which I translated to mean the frequency *should* be private but he couldn't guarantee it. We descended into the former engine room of the station, and my suit informed me atmospheric conditions were suitable for life.

Carthello removed his clear, domed helmet first, and I followed his example. "No secrets will leave this room."

"I want to call in your debt to find out who bought a shipment of core shiftgems from planet busters. I have a lot of stones I found in the derelict that were being smuggled; the Deltan I want to clear had no idea they were on board. I suspect they were snuck in, the smuggler realized he couldn't get them out *or* he was scheduled to have the ship robbed, and things didn't work out. The Deltan I'm clearing was put into stasis, and I found the core crystals in the cargo bay, disguised among the cargo—on top."

"Loaded last, after the inventory manager had finished work and was closing up."

"Yes. The Deltan is the inventory manager from what I understand. He is utterly unsuited for your line of work. He spent our quarantine period desperately learning how to fix engines."

Carthello made a gesture to respect the dead, and I mimicked him. "His first bad run, then."

"Almost his last. They were inexperienced with stasis and overdosed him with the sedative. I was able to revive him with no harm done, but it was a little testy."

"For you to say it is testy, it was a worry indeed. You became attached to this Deltan."

"I even gave him an idiotic name based on his planet so he wouldn't become a real person. It turns out I have made mistakes, but at least I can clear my conscience—and his home world—of wrongdoing. Assuming, of course, you can help me track the sale of the shipment." I set the crate down, opened it, and pulled out the invoice slip. "Amateurs."

Making use of one of his tentacles, Carthello claimed the sheet. He whistled, followed up with some hoots. "Yes, this is a trackable shipment. I can give you everything. Who. What. Where. When. And yes, the why. You are correct, these were from a planet busted shipment. The paper is imprinted. You cannot read it, but I can. They were to be used to sabotage the sovereignty of a planet."

"Cremora Delta 005-26?"

"The same. The black market operator was displeased with what he learned, why the buyer wanted the stones, and the acquisition method of the stones. The buyer requested the dirtiest stones possible. Planet busted from an inhabited world. The whole story is here on this sheet of paper, and the buyer was not aware." Carthello offered the sheet back. "That sheet and a psionic reader is all you need to prove his innocence. I suspect the man you protect is mentioned in there. One was innocent. Three were not. One had a conscience. The others didn't."

"Conscience enough to break the shiftgem crystals throughout the ship without being able to repair them?"

"And to put the one innocent into stasis so only they would pay for the millions of lives lost."

Fucking planet busters. "How much would it cost for you to transmit this data to Cremora Delta 005-26 along with the relevant information? They know I was on board the ship, and I'm prepared to take the credit for having apprehended the core crystals."

"You can be cleared readily enough. You have salvaged core shiftgems before. You are licensed to carry them on board. You verified their source, and I will draw up the documentation for you. This was not condoned by our market, and we will honor this—and make certain the planet busters responsible fall. But you will become a target."

I sighed. "When am I not a target?"

"Moreso than you already are. The planet busters will steer clear of you. You're being targeted by Veloc. But the Veloc? The instant they find you would fling yourself on a sacrificial altar to recover core shiftgems and see them properly handled? They will not rest until you fall into their clawed clutches."

I snorted a laugh. "I'd rather be romanced by one of

their cousins, but being romanced is not a *bad* thing, Carthello. Venturing through space can be lonely. I'd even bring him back from time to time."

I doubted Delta would leave his city, not with how much relief I'd seen on his face when he'd beheld his home after his harrowing adventure on the freighter. I wouldn't want to leave home after that for a while, either. Unfortunately for me, my ship was my only home.

"Women," Carthello complained. "Always wanting *romance*."

"No, that's the Veloc. I just understand there are benefits to the whole romance idea."

Some of the benefits were more enjoyable than others, but I'd learned long ago to control my hormonal impulses. Space and hormones rarely mixed well. I would need to take a cold walk through space to restore my senses—after I handled the core shiftgem issue.

Carthello chuckled. "You were always a strange one. You are wearing one of the stones, I see. No, I hear. I hear the stone singing its joy."

With my helmet off, I could dig my hand inside my suit, fish for the chain, and pull out the stone I'd put on. "Rainbow black. I wanted an accessible stone to show you."

"You will have to register that as yours. It sings, and it will not accept another owner. No matter. These stones are psycho-activated, so it is to be expected there might be a mishap. I will simply inform the authorities the stone is wiser than most and understood your intent when you secured them."

"I was going to return them to their planet of origin if that was an option. Or their people."

Carthello shook his head. "There are none left to return

the stones to. I'm sorry. But I hear the truth of your words, and they will know you had good intentions. They will mark that stone as your compensation, I'm sure. And perhaps another for a system on your ship. A stasis chamber, perhaps? I have a single-person model in stock and ready for install. You could have one ready in an hour."

I grimaced. "The price?"

"Your agreement to help with legal missions would be a sufficient price for the unit. In truth, you have rescued many of our smugglers from bad situations, and like the Veloc, we take such life-debts seriously. This would clear all debts owed to you for the lives saved, and you will be able to save more with the chamber and the stones required to operate it. You will, of course, have to set aside your pride and acknowledge the debts we owe." Carthello snickered and waggled his tentacles at me.

Bastard. "Very well. I acknowledge I have less sense than any sentient should have, resulting in me risking my life more than I should for a bunch of life-debt obsessed species. Debts owed are no longer owed for the stasis chamber, which I'll inevitably use to accumulate even more life-debts I don't wish burdening my shoulders."

"Wise, wise, wise." He held up his tentacles, and his beady lizard eyes paled to a silvery hue.

Psionic abilities came as varied as the stars, but I hadn't seen someone's eyes change color using such an ability before. One day, I might be brave enough to ask him what else he'd done on his quest to transform himself into the perfect being.

Then again, maybe I was better off not knowing.

"They will begin installation work on the stasis chamber as soon as we are finished here. They are taking it to your dock now. I have warned them your security system is impressive, and they will wait patiently for us to finish our business. They will, as they value their lives as much as they do their hearing."

I grinned, as I'd deafened a few assholes who'd thought they could mess with me and my ship. "Did they finally irritate the wrong sentient?"

"Veloc got them both after they tried to steal a hatchling."

I winced. "Having seen those claws and their teeth, I suppose they probably hadn't lasted long."

"They get annoyed when their meal kicks and screams, so no. They hadn't. They ate them both and broke the bones down to fragments as a reminder of why Veloc hatchlings are not to be stolen and smuggled."

"Noted. Do not steal adorably cute Veloc hatchings. I've seen the adolescents. They're gangly fluffs. Two had gotten into trouble and had been assigned as mules to stock my ship."

Carthello snickered. "You have earned much trust for them to allow a pair of their young to work for you. You could have easily lured them off."

"Oh, I charmed them with my engine room. Those two will be flying one day, you mark my words."

"You are a terrible influence."

"Sell me something I can actually pay for, Carthello. I feel dirty right now."

"How about a protectorate for a stolen Veloc hatchling we received? We tossed the culprit into stasis, and you can deliver the youngling back to their parents. We already promised transport."

"I'm *paying* for that?"

The operator once again laughed. “Well, you’ll be paying by capturing the attention of even more Veloc. Very well. How about a spare set of tri-color shiftgem crystals suitable for your engine? We have new stones in. They’re legal and can be registered for your engine. They’re even cheap, as you are one of the few who can actually use them well.”

“Sold, assuming my token account can cover the expense.”

“I checked it. It can more than cover the expense. You have not checked your accounts lately, I see. Your compensation was paid from Cremora Delta. Post tax, as the note says in the public record.”

“I had convinced myself they’d go the single token but restocked me route,” I admitted. “I have a fortune of stasis-frozen food on board. I’ve been eating like a queen, as has Pandora. They switched up my labels and replaced most of my cargo containers, too.”

“How inconsiderate of them, making you use your revival system for such things.”

I allowed myself an overdramatic sniffle. “The cargo containers come with unfreezing units for their goods.”

“Ah. That explains why you assumed they only sent a token. Those are not cheap units. But nice.”

“I just put the food under the scanner on the side, and it removes them from stasis. I haven’t figured out how it works yet, but it’s pretty incredible. You can even put leftovers into stasis with the one crate.”

“Your frugal heart must have wept tears of joy upon learning of that function.”

“I sobbed,” I announced with zero shame. “I sobbed real tears.”

"I bet you did. You have plenty of funds for the crystals for your engine, and I will give you them at a ten percent markup from our full expenses for their acquisition."

"That's more than fair. I was going to ask about rainbow blacks."

Carthello's many eyes focused on me. "We have some. Those are dangerous shiftgems, Viva. They can kill as easily as they can save."

"I know. I might one day use them for my engine, but they're compatible with just about everything, so I'd like a set for emergency repairs."

"I would not normally sell these. We consider them black hole acquisitions. The authorities ask for us to make sure they disappear. But we keep them in case the right owner comes around. They know this. We know this. In your hands, for your purposes, perhaps it is the best I sell them to you. I will get the authorization first. To do so, I will send them your history, and they will decide the price for the stones."

"You're really going legal."

"For some things. We will be the market the authorities know exist and will be able to operate openly. There are some lines we will not cross, like planet busting, but they will ignore other operations. We have an agreement. The spaceport will be neutral territory. Our operation will handle imports, and the legal workers will go through the main exporting section. There will be certain hours when the authorities will ignore the ships that enter via the import and do not leave through the export section of the port."

"Anything else I should know before I let a bunch of folks on my ship to install this stasis chamber?"

"There's a bounty for your pristine and living head, but

as you're aware of the Veloc chasing you, it's no concern. The Veloc are excessive when it comes to these matters. Expect to be chased—but don't worry about your ship. *That* is covered by the bounty as well. You and your ship are to come to no harm. I hope you like the idea of being romanced, because you're courting trouble."

"Do I get a free pass out of the station?"

"You do, but only because there is a bounty for information on your whereabouts. I recommend you head to Veloci Minor. Humans like yourself amuse them, and all you would have to do is tell one you're playing hard to catch. A clan would surely act as your host and entertain you until it was time for you to be appropriately hunted. Or romanced, as the case is."

"No is always an answer if I don't like the romancing, no matter how persistent Veloc think they are—or their little cousins."

"Ah, you underestimate the Veloc, Viva."

"No, they underestimate me."

Carthello cackled. "For that alone, I will find you a treasure among my wares you will adore so much you must buy it for the sake of your sanity. But first, let us attend the matter of the little Veloc. She is young, she is frightened, and she would very much like to go home."

TEN

"Guard her."

WHILE CARTHELLO and his fellow operators installed the stasis chamber in my cargo bay, taking over the corner nearest the entry to the rest of the ship, I introduced myself to the Veloc. She barely came up to my knee, and some asshole had caged her. She whistled, the cry of distress hurting my heart. Someone had made an effort to feed her, although she wore half of her food rather than eating it.

First, I needed to get the gunk out of her downy feathers, then I needed to apply the oil to keep moisture away from her skin. The work would take me hours, but I'd manage.

They would need hours to install the stasis chamber and calibrate it.

I trilled at her to catch her attention, then I introduced myself and promised I would be taking her home to her parents. Her crest snapped up, and she whistled and trilled, the equivalent of baby babble with a few words smattered in. I recognized the two important ones: pleas for her mother and father. I cooed to her and used a mix of whistles, trills, and clicks to confirm I would be taking her home to her mother and father. She waved her taloned hands at me, the claws already sharp despite her age.

While I needed to calm her several times, I managed to install the caps so she wouldn't hurt me or herself in her excitement, then I released her from the cage and eased her onto my lap. Using a damp cloth, I removed the spilled food from her feathers before taking a clean cloth and the feather oils and applying them from head to tail to help prevent her from becoming ill. Once done, I fed her properly, wearing a thick pair of leather gloves and following a pictorial guide on how to get most of the food down her gullet rather than onto her chest. She also got milk, which she drank from a bottle. I grinned at her effort to hold the metal cylinder containing her meal. I adjusted the angle so she could rest her hands on it.

She went through three before she had her fill and decided I made a safe haven, snuggling on my lap. I whistled for Pandora, who came over and sniffed at our new companion.

"Guard her," I ordered the fox.

Pandora flicked an ear, sniffed the hatchling, and assumed a position by the door. A moment later, she chittered a warning.

"Your chamber is finished. I will leave your new treasure in the hall here. I'm charging you two hundred tokens for it. I'll leave you to get your ship ready. We'll make certain we close the inner hatch before letting ourselves out."

"Take your tracker with you when you go. Fly safe."

He told me the coordinates for the new spaceport and left. I heard the interior door to the cargo bay close. A few minutes later, the gangway opened. The daredevils would hop to the dock, the sensible would retrieve the ones who misjudged their trajectory, and I'd laugh at the thought of black market operators indulging in more childish tendencies.

Ten minutes later, I transferred the hatchling to my co-captain's chair and retrieved a blanket to make a nest for her. Once done, and with Pandora standing guard, I investigated the trouble Carthello and his crew had left for me. In the hallway, I discovered a cage with a *vulpes vulpes* kit in it, and the kit cowered, staring at me with wide brown eyes. Knowing Carthello, he'd given me a boy, and he would have come from a different line than my Pandora.

I went to the nearest console near the bay, tapped in Carthello's frequency, and said, "Two hundred tokens? You're taking a loss there, sir!"

The black market operator laughed. "You're saving me a fortune in care costs, and you have a *vulpes vulpes.* Yes, I know your rules, yes, they're genetically diverse, and yes, he's a legal acquisition. He is two hundred tokens because that is what I invested to get him here. I was waiting for you to show up, and I had figured you would be due. Of course, I thought you'd show up in two or three months, but he can grow with you rather than with me. He is a life-debt gift, so you cannot refuse him."

"How the hell did I get so many life-debts?"

"That is simple. You live to save, so you do. That one remembered your lonely *vulpes vulpes* and wished to acquire companionship for her."

"Well, please pass my gratitude and whatever wishy-washy bullshit is appropriate to say to the life-debt species I tangoed with that time."

"Any other problems, Viva?"

"I wouldn't call it a problem, but I have to check after everything you did and find the trackers you inevitably hid."

"I took them with me since you asked so kindly. And anyway, it's more fun when you aren't tracked. Open a communication line with me in twenty minutes. I'll send you the safest flight path to Veloci Minor. She should be returned to her family as soon as possible."

"I can do three jumps without an engine check."

"It's two and a doozy to get there, so you'll be fine. Your rainbow blacks are in three new storage containers. The fee for the containers are included with their price. I didn't ask if you approved of the cost before charging you. You can afford it."

"For the sake of my curiosity, how much?"

"One token per, three hundred per container."

I choked on my own spit. "What the hell?"

"The authorities deemed it would be unethical to sell them when you'll be using them for derelict rescues. And the three hundred for the containers is the minimum they can sell the containers for due to trade rules."

Huh. When I thought about it, it made sense. Rainbow blacks tended to create more disasters than they averted. "Please thank them for me."

"I shall, but you will ultimately be the one deserving of thanks."

TRUE TO HIS WORD, Carthello had taken all of his trackers with him, although he'd left a few gifts in the form of information regarding the crystals I had taken from Delta's ship, supplies for the kit, enough food for the Veloc hatchling to last her through a siege, stored in nice cargo container I wouldn't be giving back. A few presents, gift wrapped with my name on them, made me roll my eyes. The insanity of black market operatives giving presents amused me, and I opened their offerings to discover a variety of lingerie in my sizes.

Bastards. I'd keep the lingerie, as it was expensive on a good day, but the taunt over the bounty would never end. I would never live down the day a bunch of idiot black market operators had gone lingerie shopping for me.

I gave it even odds that they'd send a receipt to the Veloc to add to the chaos.

The last present included a necklace, bracelet, and earrings fashioned from rainbow black shiftgem crystals, unsuitable for anything other than baubles. That would have been something Carthello would have acquired, knowing my fascination with the stone.

I would appreciate the set, aware the days of debt were over, setting us both free from the weight of obligation.

I put the jewelry box in my personal safe in my cabin before hauling my new fox kit to my navigation room, where the hatchling still slept and Pandora stood guard. I crouched, whistled for Pandora, and opened the cage. "Meet your new friend, Pandora. Carthello got him for you."

Pandora's eyes widened, and she sniffed in the cage. After a few more sniffs, she wagged her tail so hard I worried she might fall over. The kit made a soft whining noise, but he emerged from his cage and crowded Pandora, seeking shelter against her.

I couldn't blame him. The poor baby likely missed his mother, barely old enough to be weaned. I'd supplement his meat diet with milk just in case he'd been taken too early.

"You need to comfort him in your nest, okay? If he makes a mess, I'll clean your nest. We'll teach him to use the box, but for the next while, things might be a little rough."

It always amazed me how much Pandora understood. She spent a moment grooming the kit before picking him up by the scruff and carrying him to her nest in our shared cabin. She eased him inside, and I buttoned the entry hole in case of a rough takeoff. I made a point of petting them both.

The kit sniffed me, and while he whined, he accepted my touch without overt signs of fear.

Carthello must have worked with him already.

I returned to my captain's chair, opened a communication link with Carthello, and said, "Thank you. Pandora has her new friend in her nest for takeoff, and the little one is adapting much better than expected."

"We've had him for a week, and we've been passing him around. He's great outside of his cage, and I already box trained him, so you won't have many problems on that front. The cage scares him, but we needed to transport him safely, and it has a shield, gravity, and life support. In case of emergency, toss your foxes in there, activate everything, and you'll buy them three weeks of air on the setup. I know you have a suit for Pandora, but it takes time to have those made. And you can use the cage for other species."

"Bill me for that cage and put in an order for three

others like it. I'll make a wall in my cargo bay for animals. I've the space, even with the stasis chamber."

"I'll bill you at cost for the cages but not a penny more."

"Deal. The rainbow black jewelry set is beautiful. Thank you."

"You deserved something beautiful and impractical, and we'd already heard about the cargo you'd rescued that captured the attention of the Veloc. It takes one hell of a stalwart soul to pass up an opportunity to make off with that load. We valued it out of curiosity."

"How much?"

"A billion for all the crystals on board—and not the core shiftgems. I did some research."

"Are we on a secure connection?"

"We're secure."

"How did a planet of evolved *homo sapiens* get a billion tokens for that many shiftgems? Why? That's ridiculous. I thought perhaps the low hundred millions."

"The tri-color set you installed in the engine is worth fifty million on its own."

I slumped in my seat. "I ruined a fifty million dollar install?"

"You didn't ruin the shiftgems. You installed them, and the ship is working great. Your work just turned that freighter into a dream ship. Word on the wire is they want you to tune the engine more. They're in love with your install."

"I paid nowhere near as much for my set."

"Your set was paid for in part by a life-debt, Viva. They footed the majority of the bill and you paid what you could afford."

Damn it. "Again?"

"That's what you get for saving everybody. Hell, almost everyone in this station has had their asses pulled out of the fire because of you. I had a bunch of fretting operators here trying to find suitable presents. I had to agree to send a ship to Veloci Minor to send additional gifts. It's chaos."

"It's not necessary."

"Viva, you're transporting a Veloc hatchling. You just saved our asses. Again. Every last one of us owes you a life-debt for taking that hatchling off our hands. You're going to be swarmed by angry Veloc, and *you* can speak to them, unlike us. And the baby already trusts you."

"She wants her mommy and daddy."

"Yeah, we'd guessed as much. The poor thing is traumatized. We've already notified Veloci Minor about your ship. We told them about the bounty, and we specified it would be more entertaining if you were escorted to return the hatchling and set loose on the planet for the other Veloc to hunt." Carthello snickered. "We're worried about the kidnappers."

"You don't know if there are more of them."

"Or why they targeted a female hatchling."

"Fuckers."

"Agreed, agreed. Still, keep on your toes, and if a bunch of angry Veloc want to board, just hold the hatchling and get her cooing, and they'll be dancing to your tune in no time."

I could handle that. "What's the recovery cut?"

"They'll handle it, but it'll be fair."

"And your cut for giving her to me."

"We'll get our payment from the Veloc clan, no fretting there. You have the dangerous job. We just beat the shit out of the fucker and put him in stasis."

"Load him," I ordered.

"Pardon?"

"Get someone to load him into the cargo bay. I'll take him to Veloci Minor and revive him myself. And observe when he gets exactly what he deserves," I stated through clenched teeth.

"And I'll just get someone to send him over. Open your gangway. We'll tether him to something, so he doesn't go flying out into space."

"I can turn on gravity in the cargo bay, too."

"We're planning on beating him on the way to the ship. He'll be alive. Just don't expect to keep your revival statistic intact."

"Nobody kills my patients until the revival process is complete. No injuring him further. He's mine, and I will feed him to the Veloc properly. After he gets a trial. Make sure they know the fucker gets a psionic trial."

"You play dirty. You want a psionic trial, you'll get it. We should put you in for diplomatic training. The Veloc are going to be conquered if they give you an inch."

"I'll beat the Veloc if they make the hatchling cry being scary and angry. She's scared enough. You can pass that around. And bring me a weapon I can use on crabby Velocs."

"I'll leave a stun baton in your cargo bay with the corpse in the making," he promised.

"I'll even pay for it."

"I'll add it to the bill."

"My bill, Carthello. If the Veloc want to give me new self-defense toys, they can. I deserve to pay for the damned thing for not having gotten one sooner."

"All right. I'll bill you for it. Give us ten minutes, and we'll board the corpse."

I rolled my eyes. "Ten minutes sounds good. I need to check on the baby."

"Keep an eye on your security cameras, and don't lower your gangway unless you see me."

"Roger."

Shaking my head over the insanity, I got out of my seat, crouched beside my co-captain's chair, and stroked the baby Veloc's head until she woke. I cooed to her. She cooed back, reaching out with her capped claws. Having seen how Veloc snuggled with each other before, I lowered my head and presented my cheek, the closest I could do to mimic how they comforted each other.

She nuzzled me and chirped.

"I'm going to be taking you home soon, sweet baby. My friends are adding a few extra pieces of cargo, then we're leaving. I expect we will be met by your kin. You will need to coo and chirp and be a happy baby for them, all right? They'll be angry because you were stolen."

While I struggled to make the correct sounds, she cooed an acknowledgment, and she began to purr, an indication she understood my request. Cradling her to my chest, I made my way to the cargo bay entry, activating the display near the door to monitor for Carthello and his companion. Eight minutes after cutting off communications, he arrived with three other operators, who hauled a corpse and another container.

Idiots. Sighing, I lowered the gangway, wondering what the container contained. I decided against asking, instead keeping an eye on them. They tethered the corpse to one of the brackets and stacked the container with others. Carthtello placed a sheet on top, waved at one of my cameras, and bounced to the end of the gangway before jumping for the space station.

Once they were all clear, I closed the gangway and returned to my seat. I activated the comm and said, "You have some serious problems with basic math, Carthello."

He laughed at me. "Have a safe flight. You're clear to go, and we've already gotten a confirmation from the Veloc they will escort you, and you won't need your new baton, which is in the container with a few other things you'll like on the self-defense front."

"Thanks. Stay safe. I expect to see you at the spaceport, so don't get yourself killed being stupid."

"I'll see you soon enough, I'm sure. Assuming you're not romanced, of course."

"And what use would I have for romance if he isn't interested in exploring the stars with me? Get with the program, Carthello. I'm not giving up space for any mere man."

He bellowed his laughter. "Off you go, Viva. And should you be successfully romanced, I will come visit to gloat over your defeat. But to soften the blow, I'll bring you more presents."

Wicked man. Well, former man. "Fly safe."

I cut the communication off before we made fools of ourselves. I returned the baby to her nest, cooed to reassure her, and eased my ship away from the dock. The thrum of the engine startled the hatchling, how flattened her crest and cowered on the seat.

"It's okay, baby," I told her in a mix of trills, coos, and whistles. I accelerated slower than normal, keeping an eye on my precious cargo. Once I got the ship up to fifty percent throttle, I stabilized the speed, set a course for Veloci Minor, and relaxed. Using the intercom, I gave Pandora permission to roam.

Then, I scooped the hatchling up, put her on my lap, and played with her, while looking through my front window for any of the common hazards of space, trusting in my ship's systems to alert me of trouble.

ELEVEN

"It won't be comfortable, but I can hold three."

FIVE DAYS after leaving the space station, my ship squealed a warning of incoming ships. Pandora chittered a warning, and she snatched the kit by the back of his neck and fled for the safety of her nest as I'd taught her. The main display indicated I'd been located by an entire fleet of Veloc. One angry adult Veloc worried me. Ten ships worth of angry Veloc left me with few options. The communication system activated with a request to communicate. As I valued my life, I sat in my captain's chair, scooped up the baby, and settled her on my lap, sacrificing my fingers to her sharp little teeth so they would see her happy and cooing rather than distressed.

I accepted the communication, approving video communication.

A Veloc with a crimson crest, a similar shade to the hatchling's, appeared on the screen. His bright green eyes focused on my lap.

"She's fine," I announced in his language. "She was

scared when she was first recovered, and those who claimed her from the kidnapper weren't sure how to care for her, so I needed to clean and oil her feathers, but she doesn't seem to have come to any harm. They provided plenty of food for her in a mix of meat and milk. She's been digesting it fine, so I assume they were able to get suitable fare for her."

The male's crest snapped upwards. "You're fluent in our language."

"I have a great deal of time in space, so I thought it wise to learn languages. Veloci is the most challenging of the languages I've learned, but it's coming in useful."

"You use the formal form, but you are understandable. Thank you for bringing her. Do you have a safe way to be boarded or to bring her to us?"

"I don't have a suit viable for her. I can't guarantee her safety. We might be able to rig a docking. If you have suits, I can open the gangway. I can board two Veloc, maybe three in a pinch." I switched to trade, hoping the hatchling hadn't been taught other languages yet. "She wants her parents, and while she accepts food and care from me, she knows I am a transporter."

"Her parents are here, and we can get them into suits. Your gangway is safe? Can you temporarily welcome a third Veloc on board?"

"It won't be comfortable, but I can hold three. The seats for landings are not precisely comfortable for your species."

"This is fine. Her parents and a guardian would be preferred. He will not be a problem, I assure you."

I nodded. "I will open the gangway. There is a man in stasis in the cargo bay. Upon revival, he will be put on trial, and upon confirmation of guilt, he will be given to you for discipline. Or as lunch. I have no pity for those who kidnap a hatchling."

The Veloc showed me all his teeth. "Lunch sounds delightful."

I bet. "I ask that no one interrupts the revival process. I take pride in getting people through stasis revival alive, and he should stand trial for his crimes. And well, if he gets eaten by a Veloc, he earned it for stealing a hatchling."

"Precisely. We will be ready to board within twenty minutes. Her parents have never been off Veloci Minor until this flight, so they are understandably frightened."

"Please cap their claws. I'd like a ship once this is over. I did cap the hatchling's claws. I hope this is not a problem."

"It is not a problem at all. A safety issue. Has she bitten you?"

"Nothing more than play nips, and I have been careful to educate her when she becomes too rough. I have a few toys for my *vulpes vulpes* we've been playing with. Please be aware I have two *vulpes vulpes,* and one is a kit. I will introduce you once her parents have calmed."

"Your understanding is appreciated. We will bring supplies for the flight, as we eat a great deal. We will check the supplies you have brought for her and evaluate if it is suitable."

I nodded. "I will kill my engines. The easiest way is to have the experienced spacewalker attach a line and shove them over along the rope. If you need assistance, I can suit up."

The Veloc's crest lowered. "Help would be appreciated. We have suits, but we are not adept at traveling through space in these suits."

"No shame," I told him, smiling. "I'll get suited up. Let

me get her settled back into her nest. I've taught her to stay in her nest when I'm busy, so she'll be safe enough. I'll leave the communication line open so you can watch and talk with her." I cradled her while making the transition to her nest, making sure none of her feathers were bent. I took the time to coo to her and reassure her, and when she reached for me, I went through our routine so she could nuzzle me. Then I left her to stay in her nest while her kin kept a careful watch.

THE VELOC NEEDED remedial lessons in space travel, and while their inability to handle a spacewalk without issue annoyed me, I couldn't complain about their ships. I terrified the lot of them just bouncing out of my ship. I laughed at the panicked chatter before engaging my thrusters and heading for the nearest of the ships. I let myself in through their airlock, waiting for them to restore life support and gravity. I was met by three Veloc wearing spacesuits. I identified the mother by her smaller size.

"You'll see your daughter soon," I told them, gesturing for them to join me in the airlock. "Please allow me to check your suits."

All three Veloc bobbed their heads in consent, and I checked all the seams, adjusting them until satisfied. Then I ran diagnostics on all suits, confirmed their life support systems would hold for the journey to my ship, and then said, "We're good. Please seal the interior door."

"Sealed," a deep voice replied. "You are clear to open the exterior airlock."

"I will make three trips, so please leave the airlock as is until I finish. I will take the mother over first."

The mother's crest, shorter than the males, although just as colorful, flattened against her head. I understood.

My first spacewalk had terrified me, and her suit lacked thrusters. It would get her to my ship safely, and that was it.

"You will be safe," I promised, holding out my hand. "Just hold onto me, and I will get you to my ship, okay?" Once I had a hold on her, I coaxed her to the exterior airlock seal, opened it, and pointed at my open gangway. "We will jump for there, and I will guide us there. Just step out and aim for there. I will take care of the rest."

The Veloc wasted no time diving out into the open reaches of space, and I laughed at her enthusiasm. She had good aim, and I needed to do minimal adjustments with my suit to land on the gangway. I activated my magnets and held her in place. "Well done. Now we will go to the door, and you will hold onto a handle. Do not disturb the body. You will have your chance with him after his trial. The black market operators send their regards, but we request he receives a psionic trial. His guilt will be confirmed. Then you can enjoy your lunch."

"You understand how we punish those who take our children?" she asked, speaking in her native language.

"It isn't how I would do it, but it is deserved, and your laws are clear." The Veloc took their children seriously—and I wished more races did as well. "I will return with your mate next. Hold on there, and don't worry. You'll be with your daughter soon."

The Veloc made a whimpery coo, and I realized the mother cried.

I patted her shoulder and launched myself back into space to retrieve her mate.

The transfer went well, although the guardian froze at the airlock and required a few extra minutes of coaxing to step out into space. I closed the exterior hatch and secured it before shoving off the ship and directing us to the gangway.

The Veloc treated me rather like an oversized stuffed animal to be hugged for comfort until I got us into the cargo bay. Once down and attached to the metal with my magnets, I eased his hold and guided him to the other Veloc. Closing the gangway took an extra five minutes, as the three Veloc were fascinated with the process.

I expected it would be a long flight filled with curious predators causing me trouble.

I restored the life support system before activating gravity, and once everything was set up to my liking, I removed my spacesuit, set it near the stasis chamber, and went to work helping them out of theirs.

"Welcome aboard." I pointed at the body. "You'll get your turn with him, but that's the one who stole your hatchling. I offered to transport him for trial upon hearing he'd been put into stasis."

The guardian bowed to me. "You have our gratitude and life-debt."

Fucking life-debts. "I am honored. Before I take you to her, let me show you the basics and make certain she's being fed the appropriate food. She's due for her next feeding soon, so I would like to make adjustments if needed." I guided them to the appropriate storage container, pulled out one of the filled canisters, and showed it to the hatchling's mother. She tapped on the canister, her eyes slitting to a thin line. "This is good milk. From our home world, from an animal we often use to supplement our hatchlings once they are older than six weeks. Their teeth come in by then, and we must use special…" She gestured to the canister's nipple.

"Nipple," I said in the trade tongue, as I wasn't aware of the word in her language.

"Yes. And the meat?"

I pulled out one of the containers I'd already been working through, which was stasis-frozen until used. I used the container's device to thaw the food and offered it to her.

She sniffed a piece before popping it in her mouth. "This is good meat. Also from our world. Small animal, good for young to hunt as they learn. Slow. Tasty. How much you feed?"

"Would you like me to feed her while you watch?"

The parents exchanged glances, and the father nodded. "Perhaps it is for the best?"

I couldn't blame them for their uncertainty. How were they supposed to move forward with life when everything had been changed on them—and on their hatchling? "If you want to take over feeding, just tell me."

I gathered enough to feed her, tucked it under my arm, and opened the door to discover Pandora and her kit waiting. The instant the foxes caught sight of the Veloc, they both squeaked their excitement and wagged their little tails. I had no idea why the kit was excited, but Pandora yipped and bounced, her gaze locked on the Veloc.

"She loves Veloc. We kept company with one named Mystoran during quarantine, so she associates you with hunting and playing."

The mother's crest snapped up, and she cooed, bending over to meet Pandora. "Precious!"

"Her name is Pandora, and I haven't named the kit yet,"

I admitted. "I want to see his personality a little more. You are welcome to play with them during the journey."

"Thank you," the mother whispered.

I adjusted my hold on the hatchling's lunch and patted her arm. "You're welcome. Come along. Let's go see your daughter and make sure she's fed and happy."

THE HATCHLING SPOTTED her mother and father, squealed, and waved her little arms in a demand to be picked up. I obeyed, kissed the side of her muzzle, and carried her over, delivering her to her mother, who let out a piercing keen, went to her knees, and held her hatchling close.

The father made a similar sound, although he stood tall, a position I recognized as defensive and ready to guard his mate and child.

"All safe and sound, and I did my best to keep her healthy," I said in the trade tongue, hoping the hatchling couldn't understand me. "She was scared when I first got her, but she warmed to me quickly. She needed to be cleaned, and I did my best."

The Veloc father lowered his head, nuzzled his mate, and reached down to inspect the wiggling baby, ruffling her feathers and checking her little limbs. "She is well, and she grows. Her feathers are sound."

"I used an oil we had for feathers."

He nodded, leaned towards me, and pressed his muzzle to my cheek. "You have our thanks and life-debt, more than you can ever know."

I reached up and patted the side of his face, aware they appreciated touch. "It was my pleasure to escort her home. I'll leave the food here if she becomes ready for it, but I will get this fleet moving in the right direction while you comfort each other. Pandora?"

My fox arrived, carrying the kit in her mouth.

"Go to your nest with your kit, please. We'll be departing, but it will be a gentle takeoff, so you don't need the buttons."

She flicked her tail at me and trotted off to do as I asked.

"She is trained," the guardian praised, his crest rising in interest. "We have *vulpes vulpes* on Veloci Minor, but not so obedient. They are wild. Sometimes prey. They control small animal populations, things too small for us to want to hunt, and we do not allow many other predators in our territory. But the *vulpes vulpes* are an exception. Beautiful. Swift. Cunning. Scavenger and hunter."

"Her parents were born on the generational ship I was conceived on."

"You are *homo sapiens*?"

"From Andromeda."

"The last ship. Remarkable. Modified. Survivability?"

I nodded. "They didn't know what I would need on the planet, and they tried to adapt all conceived before landing for survivability. But the planet wasn't hostile, and the modifications weren't needed. That's a good thing. My parents gave me Pandora when I registered to venture through space."

"We could catch *vulpes vulpes* and teach them like your Pandora?"

"I'm sure you could—or catch a breeding pair and

domesticate them and their kits. Pandora is genetically modified for a longer lifespan and heightened intellect. I will have to get the kit tested, but it's probable he's modified, too."

"How interesting."

I gestured for the guardian to follow me, sitting on my chair, waving to the Veloc who'd waited through the entire process of reuniting parents and child. "All is well. I have a route that I was told is the most direct. Can you verify this for me?" I pressed a few buttons on my chair's console and then utilized my link to transmit the data to the Veloc. "I would like to get them back to your world as quickly as possible, obviously."

"Yes, this route is good, but the last jump gate is troublesome. We will take a five gate route. Our ships cannot handle the last gate."

Interesting. "What's wrong with the gate?"

"It has opinions. No one dies, but you may not go where you meant to. You may not even emerge at another gate. That gate will take you where you need to go. It is sentient."

My brows shot up. "The shiftgem gate is *sentient*?"

"That is what we believe. All who venture there are wise to treat it with respect. But we received word you are one with the stars. If that is the route you wish to take, we will meet you at Veloci Minor. You are in our space now, and we have many ships, and they are all hunting for those who would hunt for our hatchlings. They will not succeed in their hunts. Not now."

Interesting. "I'll take the gate. It is better for them to return to their home as quickly as possible."

"You understand."

I did. "My ship is rated for planet entry, and I'm qualified to do entry and exits, as long as you can secure me authorization to venture onto the planet."

"Consider permission to be granted. I will notify Veloci Minor of your ship's details. Fly safely, fly swiftly, and hunt well." The screen went dark, and aware of the precious cargo I carried, I eased away from the escort and began the last stage of their journey home.

Then I would put the issue of the core shiftgems to rest and go off in search of my next adventure.

TWELVE

They called her Miracle Star

I UNDERSTOOD what the Veloc had meant by the shiftgem gate possessing sentience upon arrival. While gates typically glowed, the gate leading to Veloci Minor—or elsewhere—shifted in odd patterns, patterns I determined had meaning.

"Wow," I whispered, sitting back in my seat and admiring the play of colors over the gate. The rainbow black crystal around my neck warmed, something it hadn't done since leaving the space station. I questioned the change, but I couldn't afford to worry about it.

"Aren't you something else?" I said, smiling at the latest marvel of space. "This is something you probably won't see again unless you're brave, stupid, or both."

The Veloc regarded me with flattened crests, with the exception of the hatchling, who sat on the floor and tried to chew on her father's capped claw. I learned Veloc named themselves upon reaching adulthood, and her baby name was Miracle of a Lost Crimson Star, as she'd broken free of her egg the same day the light of a dying red dwarf star had reached their world.

They called her Miracle Star as a nickname, and I loved everything about the hatchling. One day, I hoped she flew, although I suspected she'd stay safe and sound on the ground.

Her parents struggled to adapt to space, but I admired their bravery.

They would do anything to be with their hatchling and see her safely home.

I took the time to explain how shiftgem gates typically worked, and then showcased the difference. Once done, I gestured to the pulsating patterns of light. "Those are all from shiftgem crystals, and the gate is activating the various colors of gems. What the pattern means? I can't tell you. But I can tell you the gate is active." And it listened. That much I could tell from how the colors changed in reaction to my words. "We're here, so I can get you home and get your baby nestled into her bed tonight. So, like we did with the other gates, sit tight in your chair. Hold your hatchling."

Once the Veloc obeyed, I used the intercom to warn Pandora we were making a jump.

Unlike the times before, I lifted the rainbow black core shiftgem from under my shirt, lifted it up on its chain, and pressed it to my lips, hoping it might somehow communicate the importance of my cargo to the gate. I let it fall, and the stone's warmth strengthened, spreading rather than growing hotter.

How strange.

Without knowing what the gate would do, I activated all thrusters, which would enable me to hover in any environment—even if the gate shot me directly into Veloci Minor's atmosphere. Then, I increased the rear thrusters to enter the gate and activated the shiftgem crystals to initiate the jump.

The gate's colors shifted to mimic that of the rainbow black, and the stomach-lurching sensation of jumping took hold. The next minute, I appreciated my foresight.

The gate hadn't sent us through space, but into the mid-atmosphere of a planet. Alarms squealed on my ship, and I slammed buttons and adjusted thrusters to restore forward motion. One by one, the warnings quieted, and my ship registered the atmospheric conditions and adjusted to them.

"And the next time someone tells me the gate has a mind of its own, I will absolutely believe them," I announced. I flipped a switch, scanned for communication lines, and identified a traffic controller frequency, which I tuned into. Rather sheepishly, I identified my ship, informed traffic control of a jump gone rather wrong, and requested direction.

A rather amused traffic controller welcomed me to Veloci Minor, informed me they had already been notified we were attempting to use their cantankerous gate, and gave me permission to land at the nearest landport located a five minute flight at minimal throttle. They gave me a new frequency and ordered me to queue in for landing, but to expect preferential treatment due to the nature of my arrival.

Three minutes later, the traffic controller at the landport scrambled to get a free runway open, but after a brief conversation, I assured them I could use any pad large enough for my vessel. While doubtful, the Veloc instructed me to a cargo copter pad, and I eased the ship over, engaged the hover functionality, and dropped her down in the center of the pad. I killed the engine, slumped in my seat, and groaned. "That was a nightmare scenario."

In my true fashion, I'd refused to accept names of my living cargo with the exception of the hatchling, as Miracle Star needed to hear her name and enjoy affection. Her mother trilled a laugh. "It was interesting."

Damned Veloc. The instant they'd gotten beyond their fear, they had thrown themselves into the whole flying experience with enthusiasm. If they asked me to go through my ship one more time, I would lose my mind.

I pointed my hand in the general direction of the doors. "Please go home but leave the body so I can revive him. You're welcome, I am honored to have enjoyed your company, and I appreciate your life-debt."

The father chuckled, as did the guardian. To my amusement, they did leave, and I opened the gangway from my seat, flipping on the security cameras to monitor the Veloc. They eyed the kidnapper, but beyond some hissing, they left his body alone.

It would do. Weary from the travel and on edge from the untraditional planetary visit, I pressed the intercom and said, "Pandora, stay in your nest, please. It is not safe yet."

I trusted her to stay and keep her new friend close. Rising to my feet, I followed in the Veloc's wake to discover what new forms of trouble waited for me.

IF THE VELOC gave me one more gift, I would lose my mind. It had started with the mother's sister, who'd keened, flung herself at me, and worshipped the ground I stood upon, wrapping herself around my legs while she wailed. At a loss, I bent over and stroked the Veloc's crest, reassuring her in her tongue and thanking her for her gratitude.

When she finally rose, she removed a gem from her crest and pressed it into my hand, begging me to accept it, and that she would adjust the setting so it could be a bauble suitable for my crest.

I recognized a shiftgem crystal when I saw one, and she'd given me a beauty of a pitch black stone. At a loss of why she would give me something so precious, I thanked her.

Her tenuous hold on her emotions frayed, and she keened more, although another Veloc intervened before she could trap me again. With the crystal in hand, I realized the entire clan had been waiting at the landport with a prayer in their hearts and a plea for some miracle on their breath.

Somehow, the shiftgem gate had understood the true need, of the family waiting for word and not knowing if or when we would arrive.

The gate had understood the true meaning of mercy, doing what it could to help those who suffered. I would need many hours to think through the ramifications of its compassion.

More Veloc approached and swarmed the parents and hatchling, and with some help from the self-assigned guardian, I dodged the more aggressive displays of affection. More shiftgem crystals made their way into my hands, my pockets, and my hair, clipped into place by several older females, who said nothing but offered nuzzles to go with their gift.

Once the procession eased, I asked the guardian, "What's going on?"

"You are a sister of our clan now, and they welcome you with a crystal each—a bauble we wear. It is a life-debt they cannot repay in this moment, so they do what they can. We had lost hope for her return."

"He took her a long way from home and chose poorly where to sell her. He picked the wrong black market, and he will pay for his choice. And if you're wise and make sure he doesn't come to harm until his trial, you may be able to hunt any accomplices."

"That will make it easier to control the clan."

"Are you prepared to imprison him?"

"We're prepared."

"Then I'll begin the revival process. If you have a doctor capable of treating humanoids, it would be useful. My medical knowledge is limited, and let's just say the operators gave him a beating. I'd like him to stay alive."

The guardian turned, and trilled, chirped, hooted, and clicked a request for the appropriate doctor and a holding cell. When he finished, I retreated to the ship, and he accompanied me.

Without me asking, the Veloc snagged the man and removed the cable tethering him to my cargo hold. "Will this be painful?"

I chuckled. "Considering I won't be giving him any painkillers for his injuries, yes. And there will be quite some time while he thaws and his nerves are firing where I simply won't give a damn. I usually try not to be cruel, but this is deserved. But I won't have him killed without a trial."

"That is because you are just and fair, excellent traits more people could use. But vicious enough to do unpleasant but necessary things."

"Let's just get him revived before the clan of angry predators realizes they're angry. A corpse can't stand trial."

THE REVIVAL PROCESS went better than expected. The black market operators had opted to use minimal sedatives for the procedure. When he realized he was surrounded by Veloc ready to eat him alive, he confessed his every sin. As I possessed common sense, I'd begun recording the activity in the revival room, beginning the moment I started the revival.

He went into my book as yet another survivor. The Veloc carted him off to stand trial. His confessions might save his life, although he would never spend another moment free. Veloc law made it clear: death or enslavement were the prices paid for kidnapping a defenseless hatchling.

She hadn't had her teeth yet when she'd been stolen from her nest, and she'd lacked the strength to use her sharp claws.

I opted to stay around for the trial, as I found it difficult to refuse the clan's requests to meet every member of their family. Had I known the clans took kin seriously, and that half the fucking planet had some form of relationship or life-debt to members of Miracle Star's clan, I would have run away.

As the newest member of said clan, with the threat of a thousand wailing Veloc to pay if I refused the honor, I learned the entire species had a serious problem with hair and feathers. I went from a *homo sapiens* to a humanoid peacock. As I lacked feathers of my own, Miracle Star's parents plucked some of theirs and had them woven into my hair. A fortune of shiftgem crystals joined the feathers, tinkling whenever I moved my head. As the Veloc understood I needed to wash my hair, they put most of the gems into a headpiece I could take off at my whim. After the first day, I accepted the reality of life until I escaped Veloci Minor: unless in the home they'd assigned me or on my ship, I would be wearing the jewels.

Or on a hunt. Apparently, the Veloc understood wearing a bazillion pounds of crystals while running around a jungle failed to result in anything other than my humiliation.

At least they didn't make me actually *run* through the jungle. They provided a rather predatory mount, which reminded me of a giant lizard with nasty claws, a nastier temperament, and a healthy fear of the Veloc. As such, it tolerated the saddle and me riding it, and it mostly behaved.

A month after reviving the bastard, he got a trial—a remarkably fair one with four different psionic practitioners *and* a psychic. Until that moment, I hadn't realized there were lines separating psionicists and psychics, instead thinking they were just different terms for the same thing.

It had something to do with how they manipulated the mind and physical state of those around them, but beyond that, I failed to understand the differences. Maybe one day I would wrap my head around it. For the sake of my sanity, I hoped not.

The last thing I needed in my life was a crystal clear view of the universe's many evils.

At first, the man had tried to talk his way out of the kidnapping, but all five of those with mental powers called him out on it. When the truth became murkier, the psychic tended to identify the lies the easiest while the psionicists were able to eventually locate the truth itself.

At first, he claimed he had found her on her own and rescued her.

It was well enough Miracle of a Lost Crimson Star couldn't reach the bastard. She hissed and swiped her capped claws at him in protest of his claim. In a way, I wished the trial lacked translators.

The hatchling learned a lot of the evils of the universe. The illusion of safety her parents had attempted to create continued to shatter. I had faith in Miracle Star, however.

The next time someone crossed her, I suspected she'd be leaving a lot of blood in her wake. When she'd been taken, her teeth hadn't grown in sufficiently to defend herself, and her claws hadn't been large enough to do much damage. Time had worked its magic, and she'd grown into her status as a predator.

That, plus her parents worked to teach her how best to kill any who tried to take her from their nest again.

The trial took three days, after which he received the choice of being the target of a hunt or enslavement in service to the Veloc he had crossed. The choice had come at the price of outing his accomplices, who would all stand trial and face death or enslavement as well when caught.

He chose the hunt, which put me in the uncomfortable position of being his transport, as everyone believed I would treat the bastard fairly if he *did* reach my ship. I'd accepted the verdict and offered my cooperation with a sigh and a condition: one of the other Veloc clans would guard my ship while I participated in the hunt.

Winning even more adoration from the Veloc hadn't

been part of my plan, but I accepted it with yet another sigh.

The bastard deserved a fate worse than death, but at least if I caught him, he'd receive a merciful end. The trial ensured the Veloc no longer understood the concept of mercy.

They desired his screams as much as his blood.

I COULD, when the mood struck me, be an irredeemable asshole. As part of my scheme to join the hunt but offer my ship should he escape, I escorted the bastard to my vessel and showed him what point he needed to reach if he wanted to leave Veloci Minor alive. I used a piece of tape on the open gangway to mark his goal.

Then, borrowing from Carthello and making use of one of the presents he'd given me, I slipped a tracker into his clothes and used my link to activate it.

The ten minute head start wouldn't save him, not from me—or the jerk of a mount I'd be using.

In a game of predators, only the cunning and wise emerged the victor. I meant to prove I could be both, and I'd only cheat a little in the process. Armed with a rather nasty rifle, one I'd used several times eliminating pirates from the derelicts they'd created, I joined the Veloc, who'd decided to treat the hunt as a family affair.

Miracle of a Lost Crimson Star wore her first gem, a bright red one the match of my tail, as a memento of her first clan hunt.

As the weakest link of the lot, the Veloc thought it

would be amusing to give me a two minute head start. I admired their confidence. Of course, a Veloc could run at least twice as fast as a human, and if he took the most direct route, he had a thirty minute jog to reach my ship. The bastard of a mount, assuming he did as I told him, would catch up in less than five minutes, as it could outrun even a Veloc.

I'd either get kicked out of the clan for being a bastard or worshipped for my prowess, cunning, and willingness to cheat when it came to preventing a torturous death.

The fool should have chosen enslavement. He would have been given to another clan, treated well enough, and died of old age or some illness rather than suffering through hours of agony and terror. And when enslaved, had he cleaned up his act, he might not have even remembered he belonged to the Veloc, who took their honor seriously.

There was no honor in abusing the enslaved for them.

At the two minute mark, with my rifle ready to go, I sent my beast off with a tap of my heels. The scaled bastard had a name, but I didn't use it, as I refused to become attached to the grouchy lizard with a hatred of all living things. I opted to pretend I wasn't going to cry when I had to leave the planet behind. No, the real damned fool was me.

Even trying to dodge names, my heart refused to obey the rules I'd set. No names, no attachments.

It turned out my traitorous heart didn't give a shit about names. Delta had cracked through that barrier first, making room for an entire clan of murderous feathered freaks who wanted to eat a human for having kidnapped one of their hatchlings. I couldn't blame them for that.

I kept reminding myself the Veloc would not show him a scrap of mercy, and it might take them days to decide to stop playing with their prey. The bastard wouldn't reach my ship alive, and everyone except him knew it.

The kidnapper still believed he could outsmart an entire planet of predators—predators who would gang together in a united front when it came to their hatchlings.

I could already hear the Veloc from other clans moving through the thick trees, watching and waiting.

If Miracle of a Lost Crimson Star's clan didn't catch him, they would. Nothing in their rules or agreements barred other clans from interfering. I'd been among them long enough to understand the truth. The one Veloc guarding my ship would, assuming their prey made it to my ship, preserve the law.

But every other Veloc on the planet sought out justice with zero care of mercy.

Making use of my link, I fixed on my target, which informed me my prey hadn't made it all that far. I directed the mount over, around and through thick groves of trees, pushing aside moss-laden vines as needed or flattening myself to the lizard's spiny back. It took me three minutes to locate him, and in that time, I'd gained several feathered shadows.

A few hooted calls, meant to mimic birds, informed me they tracked me as much as my prey. I almost chuckled at the realization they forgot I could speak their language.

They worried I might get lost in the jungle.

They'd be getting a rather nasty surprise.

At some point in his flight, the bastard had decided climbing a tree might save him. I suspected he'd given up attempting to run or hoped to catch his breath. When I treated him like one of the pirates who murdered crews for cargo, I found it simple enough to set my rifle in place on my shoulder, take aim, set it to silent mode so I wouldn't disturb the wildlife or hurt the ears of the nearby Veloc. I made use of a laser sighting to get a bead on his head before finishing the job with a single armor-penetrating round.

The bastard hadn't even realized he'd been found before he fell from the tree and hit the ground. As I had no interest in examining a human's brain matter, I turned the beast so it wouldn't get some rounds, lowered my rifle, lifted the barrel, and blew off imaginary smoke. "Point to me," I announced. "Rules are rules—and my rules say we don't eat the corpse of a humanoid I shot, so one of you can tie the body to my saddle. I'll pay for it, but he'll be returned to his planet of origin for a proper burial, along with a copy of the verdict and that he had a clean, quick end."

In other courts, the bastard would have rotted in prison for years before facing execution for the crime.

Mercy had won, and I wouldn't blemish my track record despite disappointing a bunch of predators.

An emerald crested Veloc emerged from the underbrush and eyed the body before regarding me with interest.

Bugger. Thc bounty clan. As all the Veloc I'd met spoke trade, I said, "I'm not available for recovery right now. You're part of Mystoran's clan, right?" I gestured in the direction of his crest. "You're the same color. Sort of?"

"Yes, we are. We arrived before the trial, and as we do not interfere in such things, we have bided our time." The Veloc went to the body, turned, and gave it a single, hard kick, careful not to use his claws. "You are a strange creature. Disturbingly ethical."

"I've been around you Veloc long enough to know you play with your food when angry, and there are a *lot* of angry Veloc around right now. I didn't want to try to sleep knowing he'd spend days screaming before being put out of his misery. It doesn't fix anything."

"It does not. In that, you are right." The Veloc snagged the body by the leg and dragged it over to my beast. Rather than tie it to the saddle, he whistled a command, and the lizard wrapped the body in its tail. "No rope required. I will provide escort. You will want to put this into stasis before he rots."

I activated my link to get a direction for my ship, and I pointed the correct way. "My ship is there."

"Then we shall go there. Your clan will catch up soon."

Sure enough, within three minutes, I had a rather unamused audience of Veloc, although most of their ire was focused on the emerald crested visitors.

Rather than engage with them over the situation, I kept urging the lizard from hell along, doing my best to keep from twisting around to stare at the body. Almost forty minutes later, mostly due to a bunch of Veloc insisting they posture and show off their feathers, we made it back to my ship.

"There are body bags in the utility closet in the hallway. Can you get one for me? I'd rather not have this asshole leak all over my ship."

The guarding Veloc hooted a laugh, went into my ship, and brought one of the leak-proof bags I kept for when things went bad on a salvage. I got off the lizard, and as I didn't trust him not to go running off at his whim rather than mine, I gave the reins to the nearest Veloc. With a little help from two of the calmer Veloc, I got the bastard stuffed into a bag and went to play with my new stasis chamber.

As I didn't have a living body to worry about, I got to skip an hour of setup, got some help from the Veloc to shove him, bag and all, into the chamber, sealed it up, and froze him in stasis for the journey to his home world.

Pandora and her kit waited at the door into the cargo bay, and they wagged their tails. Smiling, I went to give them treats and praised them for being good. Then, as I wanted to see how long it would take me to ditch the corpse on his own world, I went to my navigation room to discover I had a rather handsome guest lounging in my chair, and he wore a pair of jeans and a rather smug smile.

"Okay, you can tell me your name now." I took my time enjoying the view. "As this is my ship, anything that boards without my permission becomes mine." As I'd made up a lot of rules since joining the Veloc clan, I said, "It's a new rule. I just made it up, but I'll have it registered onto my list of rules guests must abide by."

Delta grinned. "And here I thought I'd have to rescue you."

I blinked. "Why do I need to be rescued?"

"You have been on Veloci Minor for a month, Viva."

"Well, yes." I eyed my hands, which had gotten a rather displeasing amount of blood on them. "I foolishly decided to stay for the trial, and the Veloc are utterly convinced the world will end if they can't shower me with general appreciation. I just had to mercy kill some idiot who thought it was a good idea to kidnap a Veloc hatchling."

"Yes, there are videos of you cuddling with the hatchling, which is making the rounds through every Veloc clan in the universe. It's become insanity. If it hadn't been for the hatchling's clan having first rights to claim you for their clan, there would be a planet-wide brawl to have you right now."

"They take their hatchlings seriously. I'm just pissed off I'd just gotten to unload most of my damned life-debts to end up with an entire fucking *planet* worth of them. It's completely unfair."

Delta chuckled. "My name is Lucas, but I've found myself growing rather fond of you calling me Delta."

I foresaw myself becoming rather confused on what to call the man in the future. "Lucas? That's it? It's just Lucas?"

"I have a family name, and I have two middle names because my parents couldn't decide which collection of bland Earth names to give me. It's a tradition. Lucas Alexander William Davenport is my complete name. My family likes trying to keep some Earth traditions alive, mostly through how they name us. Lucas came from a list of common Earth names before the generational ships departed the planet. Alexander and William are the names of world leaders from Earth. Davenport is our original family name. As I have a life-debt owed to you, my family kicked me out, along with my cousins, so we're here to pick a fight with your clan."

I foresaw a great deal of posturing. As I'd accepted the Veloc lived to posture, I heaved a sigh. "Wait here, charm my foxes, and let me get cleaned up. I'm inappropriately dressed—and I'm wearing the blood of an asshole kidnapper, which isn't a good look on anyone. For the moment, I'm still calling you Delta. You just don't feel like a Lucas to me right now."

"Call me anything you'd like. Also, that blood is an excellent look on you. He deserved his fate. And frankly, you gave him a lot more mercy than he deserved."

"Perhaps so, but I would rather be merciful than cruel, and I know just how many angry Veloc all wanted a pound of flesh. He wouldn't have had enough flesh to go around, so they would have gone the paper cut before dismemberment route, I'm sure. Wait here unless one of the other clans asks you nicely to go to the visitor center, in which case, go to the visitor center. They'll provide one of those bastard mounts to get you there unless they really hate you, in which case, good luck. It's a long walk."

THIRTEEN

Their life-debt claim trumped everything else

I SHOULD HAVE KNOWN I would become a doll for the amusement of my clan. As one of the nosy Veloc with overly good hearing had heard me claim Delta as my property, they'd decided there was one acceptable resolution: the clans would wage war over who got to keep him, and my clan would encourage the fireworks.

My clan refused to give up ownership of my person, and their life-debt claim trumped everything else. Delta, on the other hand, classified as loose property, free to be captured and dressed up by the victorious clan. As a general rule, Veloc engaged in rather rough battles over loose property while the source of their interest observed. In Delta's case, he basked in the attention while Veloc parents attempted to charm him into their clan through the ruthless use of wretchedly adorable hatchlings.

As I'd called property rights first, I got a dose of the hatchling love, too. For the most part, Miracle of a Lost Crimson Star owned my lap, although she'd permit other hatchlings to join her for a nap. Her favorite young suitor, a yellow crested male, pitched a fit whenever his parents tried to separate them.

According to his mother, he'd been inconsolable when she'd disappeared, and everyone expected they would become a pair upon reaching adulthood, although knowing both hatchlings, they'd draw out the chase to annoy everyone around them.

"So, how is your no-name policy working out for you?" Delta asked.

"Miserably, apparently." I scratched Miracle Star along her stubby crest, and she melted into a purring puddle. "I tried not to name you, but then I named you something utterly stupid, and you're fine with it. Now you're named, and you're not going away anytime soon, are you?"

"I'm not, and I'll admit I'm relieved you realized this. I was brought up from a young age to understand romancing is serious business. Of course, no one bothered to stop and explain how the hell to actually go about it, so I'm taking it a day at a time. So far, it's been seven days, the Veloc are *still* fighting over property rights, and Mystoran's father called *my* father because it's looking like they're going to turn this nonsense into a planet-wide festival. What did you *do*?"

"Why are you blaming me?"

"Well, they're fighting over me so they get to claim relations with you. Every damned Veloc on this planet has claimed they owe you a life-debt at this point."

"All I did was play transport, Delta. That's it. A black market operator told me they had a Veloc hatchling who needed to go home, and I volunteered. I *speak* Veloci, and speaking Veloci is really important when you don't want the Veloc to eat you alive for having their hatchling."

"First, most Veloc understand they tend to eat those who take their hatchlings. Not only did you willingly agree to transport their hatchling, you fixed her feathers, fed her properly, and comforted her. She's not terrified of space travel unlike most Veloc. It takes them twice as long to adapt to space compared to *homo sapiens*."

"Like her parents. They were terrified. Their guardian took a lot of coaxing to get to make the short trip between ships. Some species just don't adapt well."

"Yeah. To complicate matters, frightened Veloc tend to become violent, so you're considered to be either the bravest human to ever explore space or the dumbest. After how you tricked the Veloc out of their kill, they're going with brave and ridiculously clever. You shocked them."

"I cheated." The tracker had become common knowledge after a few hours, as I'd gotten tired of the posturing and told them I hated to lose and how else was I supposed to beat a bunch of living, breathing murder machines? "Calling them living, breathing murder machines hadn't been my best moment."

"But accurate. Hilarious, too. You'd gotten so flustered. You don't handle praise well." Delta reached over and moved one of the many crystals away from my eyes so I wouldn't bat at it and get yet another scrape on my knuckles fighting with my jewelry. "At least Mystandor's clan canceled the bounty after learning what was going on here. It'd become a literal bloodbath if they were fighting over the bounty on top of my property rights. Worse, my father will probably bring my mother and my birth certificate and tell them to take me. I'm a rather large source of stress for them right now. I'm supposed to be training to help govern the planet, and I'm off on Veloci Minor, being told I need to start making attempts to romance you. Frankly, they're fighting because they understand I'm the definition of hopeless."

My eyes widened. "You're your planet's *heir*?"

"Yes and no. Cremora Delta worlds are run through a type of planetary congress. A quarter of the congress is hereditary, with one of the hereditary members leading the congress. My father is the current planetary leader by vote. I'd been sent on the freighter to secure our shiftgem crystals. We're getting a spaceport of our own rather than relying on the Cremorans to handle our imports and exports. They love the idea because they have to help the Veloc. Let's just say they're not ideal at interplanetary trade. Having us become more independent is a good thing."

Piece by piece, things began to make sense.

How better to prevent change than create a catastrophe for the congress, resulting in the expansion project? I could readily understand how and why those on board the ship would betray Delta—and want to preserve his life. If Delta took the blame, his father fell, too.

I reached into my shirt and retrieved the rainbow black core shiftgem I'd taken from the stash. "Did they tell you what this is?"

"They did. The ship's mechanic, not that he was good at his job, had smuggled core shiftgems from a planet busting operation. They discovered everything had been a ruse. The straw lots where I drew first? Planned."

I could guess. "The lots were all marked the same?"

"They were."

"Why save you? So your dad could take the fall?"

Delta shrugged. "I don't know. Remorse, maybe? *I* haven't done anything wrong. I'm notorious about being a stickler for the rules. Maybe they realized nobody would believe I would smuggle core shiftgems? My father received a comprehensive report from your associates. The authorities overseeing shiftgem production are opting to give the gems to our world, as there were no survivors from the original operation. We have no idea what to *do* with them, which I think played a part in their decision to give them for us. We have a vault, and they're going there for now."

"Stasis revival units and stasis chambers," I replied. "Medical equipment. Core shiftgems are all about the formation of life. They work best when in those types of machines. You could become a leader in medical instrument research with access to those shiftgems. They're in so many sizes."

"And colors. It's a thought, and I'll talk to my father about it."

"What will you talk to me about?"

I recognized Klearno's voice, and I turned to regard the man, struggling to keep from grinning at his exasperated tone.

"The core shiftgems. Viva recommends we put them to use in medical equipment."

"I'll add that to the agenda. Why is it I got a call informing me you were being abducted by a Veloc clan?"

Delta pointed at me. "It's her fault. She made a statement regarding unattended property on her ship belonging to her, and it turned into a planet-wide brawl over property rights. She's been adopted by the Crimson Crests, and the other clans are all wanting a piece of me because they can claim kin relations that way. They have decided we're a pair, and I've been instructed to get busy with the romancing, Dad."

Delta's father snickered. "And you have no idea what you're doing because your first love was a book. About butterflies, to be specific. Thank you for bringing Miracle of a Lost Crimson Star home. We were prepared to get involved with her recovery, but we have little in the way of offense. We're set on the defense, especially with the help of the Veloc and Cremorans. We've got a long way to go in everything else. Please forgive my son for his lack of romancing skills, bringing much shame to our Veloc cousins. We figured he was a lost cause. He's always preferred books and learning over women."

I understood Delta well enough, then. "I learned to speak Veloci from education modules. I share his condition. It's non-lethal, but it interferes with normal relationships with sentients."

"Thus your reluctance to learn names of those you have to share close quarters with?"

I sighed and bowed my head. "It just turns out I renamed him to be Delta, and he seems to like it."

"He never liked being called Lucas anyway. He bitched and moaned it always sounded like someone was calling him an ass. Nicknames are used on our world, and I'm sure most will start calling him Delta soon enough, especially as he seems to like it. We'll save calling him an ass for when he's being one. So, Lucas."

I snickered at the emphasis on the second syllable of his name. "You've done something to upset your family, Delta."

"I didn't write, I didn't call, I ran off with the first ship willing to take me and a few Veloc friends here, and I may have walked out of a meeting when word came down the wire I needed to get to the landport. Oh, that reminds me. Do you know someone named Carthello?"

"I do. Why?"

"He sent the ship when we inquired on transport to Veloci Minor. He had a message?"

Oh, boy. "He's calling in another damned life-debt again, isn't he?"

Delta's shoulders shook from his effort to keep from laughing. "You saved him from being eaten by a clan of angry Veloc, as *he* was supposed to transport Miracle Star home."

That explained a lot. Carthello had his defenses, but he would not have appreciated tangoing with an enraged Veloc clan. "But I'd just gotten rid of the last one!"

"You'll live. That's what he told me to tell you when you said something like that. He's rather… unique. I was afraid to ask."

My eyes widened. "Carthello escorted you here personally?"

"He said he was on his way to his new spaceport and wanted to make sure you, the hopeless female that you are, had at least *some* chance of securing a male who might be trained to enjoy going into space as much as you do. I'm at the stage where I am coming to terms with spending most of my time in space rather than safely on a planet where my father can yell at me for skipping out on meetings."

Delta's father sighed. "We'd already discussed this, boy. The planet *needs* representatives who are actually willing to go off without bribes, threats, and extensive amounts of cajoling involved. We sent you to get the shiftgem crystals because I caught you sneaking around the landport trying to get a closer look at the ships. You can go adventure in space as long as you do so safely. Anyway, you have brothers. If you get lost—again, mind you—I'll just sacrifice one of them to the planetary council."

"Ouch, Dad. I'm hurt."

According to Klearno's snort, he didn't believe his son to be capable of being hurt by something as minor as parental displays of displeasure. "No, you're going to be hurt when the Andromedan delegation arrives, as I informed them one of their pristine *homo sapiens* adventuring women had been adopted by a Veloc clan and was being courted by my son."

Miracle of a Lost Crimson Star cooed her amusement and settled in on my lap to take a nap with her best friend, who'd dosed off at least an hour ago. "Are you courting me, Delta?"

"Apparently?"

"Is this what romancing is, then? We get to sit around, be fed delicacies by a bunch of bickering feathered murder machines, and listen to your dad lament about his latest life issues?"

Delta narrowed his eyes. "If this is romancing, it's not bad. I prefer learning how to take your engine apart and put it back together again, honestly. That was a challenge. This is enjoyable, but it's not at all challenging."

"We're being spoiled," I informed him. "There is plenty of time to take engines apart and put them back together. We have to take the spoiling very seriously, as there's little room for such luxuries in space." I thought about my new collection of storage containers. "Well, before Mystoran's clan and Carthello got a hold of my cargo bay, there wasn't a lot of room for luxuries in space, but they spoiled me. Maybe I should give you the kit so you can have a *vulpes vulpes* of your own. Then Pandora can own you *and* your kit. And me. And everything she sees." I pointed in the general direction of the latest group of Veloc to have claimed responsibility for my foxes. In reality, my foxes had taken over yet another clan with their furry charms. "They're going to learn a lot of bad habits, but we'll have time in space to teach them how not to destroy everything. And they're smart. They train quickly. We'll have to get the kit his own nest, though. The nest is important for his safety during takeoffs and landings—or when things get sketchy on the ship. And before we can leave, we need to get his adult spacesuit made and several suits for while he's growing. We'll also have the cage Carthello gave me for emergencies, although we'll be stocking a few of those for odd rescues."

"Is romancing spoiling, then?"

I considered his question. "I don't know. If I spoil you and you spoil me, is that romancing?"

Delta's father heaved a sigh. "Veloc tend to view romancing like that, with the general expectation that after the first stage of romancing is complete, the pair will become a permanent couple. Then the nature of the romancing changes, in that they'll still spoil each other, but they're spoiling each other with additional benefits. Those benefits can result in infants of the appropriate species. You two are currently serving as the bed of the product of various successful romancing attempts. While I can't speak for Viva's parents due to their status as generational ship inhabitants, you are the first product of a successful romancing attempt. Your mother made me spend two years romancing her before she took pity on me. I had to recruit help from the clan for tips and tricks on how to stop screwing everything up. It didn't work to plan, but your mother took pity on me after a while. She thought it was sweet I'd put in the effort and tried."

"It's good to know where I got my inability to handle romance from. Thanks, Dad."

"You're welcome."

As I wanted to hear more about the man's failed romancing attempts, I hooted and whistled for Mystoran, who trilled a call back and loped over from one of the numerous groups of bickering Veloc. "Hey. How bad was Delta's dad at dating his mother?"

"They dated?" the Veloc replied in a disgusted tone. "It was shameful. A shame on our clan, a scourge upon his family! Only luck saved him from losing. Delta's mother? A patient soul. So patient. Please do us all the honor and favor of sparing us from such nonsense. As we heard the disheartening questions for clarification, allow me to illuminate you. Romancing is whatever you want it to be. If you wish to build engines together and use this to cement your family, then build engines. Explore space. Enjoy the spoiling as you can. The point is to build a family together, not to adhere to the standards of any one other couple. Delta is not his father, and we thank the stars that you are not his mother. You are cut from an entirely different cloth than these weak little Deltans who just learned there are wonders to behold among the stars."

"Says the Veloc, from a species notoriously bad at adapting to space travel," I replied.

"Ah, we may be bad at it, but we understand the worth of such adventures—and we go as needed. The Cremora Deltans? Oh, they have far to go. You should teach them. Then you can fly often and do what you do best, rescuing novice space travelers from themselves and disaster."

Damn. The Veloc had me dead to rights. "But will they whine when I take him with me?"

"Only if you don't bring him back at agreed upon intervals. They will annoy you from time to time, but you will accept the price you must pay to keep both of your clans from whining severely or attempting to follow you."

I foresaw a great deal of trouble and stowaway hatchlings hungering for exploration. I would need to keep spacesuits suitable for Velocs—and get at least two chairs compatible with both species. "How often do you need to return to your home world?"

"Once every five or six years should suffice," he replied.

Delta's father cleared his throat.

"I don't think he agrees with you. Five or six years does give ample time for exploration, but my ship doesn't stock that long in supplies. You can get across most of space, with the assistance of the gates, in six to eight months. Perhaps you should tentatively offer every six months for a period of two months. There's something to be said about being on a planet for a while. But after two months, you'll long for a good outing."

"Okay. Six months with two month visitations before I leave again, Dad."

"That's a little more reasonable. Why don't we try for three times a year with one of those visits being during one of our major holidays?"

It amused me that Delta's father had already come to terms with his son going out into space. I would need to come to terms with Delta wanting to venture out into space with me. Then, I realized I had a major problem on my hands. I stared at Mystoran with wide eyes. "I think I'm going to need a bigger ship."

"Or an interior overhaul," the Veloc agreed. "I'm sure

we can come up with something. Little Cousin, might I make a suggestion?"

"Sure."

"Challenge the Veloc to design the best ship possible for you and your lady to venture into the unknown in search of the lost. May the best design win. Then she can transform her ship into one you will both be pleased with. You will surely have a nest here and on our world, but your true nest will voyage between the stars."

Huh. Mystoran had good ideas. "You should do that. The Veloc might not be great at traveling, but their ships seem to be good."

"We are great designers. We are not so good at flying the things we design. It is one of our few flaws."

"The only thing flawed was your hunting tactics," I replied.

Mystoran bowed his head, flattened his crest, and whistled his despair. "You have chosen a cruel female, Little Cousin."

"I like her just as she is."

FOURTEEN

They adored each other to the point of death

ONE YEAR, three months, and twenty days after landing on Veloci Minor, I said goodbye to my old life and welcomed in the new. I'd been warned the Veloc took romancing to extremes, but nobody had told me they viewed weddings as the most important ceremony in one's life. In the tradition of the Veloc, I started my day with a head-to-tail grooming, where they decked me out in a ridiculous number of jewels and a white dress. Typically, they dressed in the color of the clans, but despite over a year of bickering, Delta had dodged being claimed. I expected he'd lose that battle soon enough, and his clan of cousins would win that war.

They adored each other to the point of death, something the Veloc respected.

Sometime during the preparations, I'd learned white had been a tradition sourced from Earth, although nobody quite understood the purity angle. Keeping my dress white for the ceremony would test the patience of the Veloc. The latest batch of hatchlings adored me, tended to follow me in flocks, and had a dress-destroying habit of spitting up fur, feather, and bone while they grew used to eating live prey.

At least they no longer needed milk, which presented a whole different spit up problem.

Miracle of a Lost Crimson Star had been one of the easier hatchlings to raise, and I'd done well not overfeeding her, thus avoiding most of the problems. The hatchling had grown into a fledgling, and she'd won the right to carry rings and flowers in another human tradition. As nobody really understood the point of the flowers, we'd ended up dressing the waist tall Veloc in a dress covered with them.

She would steal hearts with her adorable attire.

"Humans are strange," I informed Delta's mother, a woman who preferred to be called Mom and refused to give me her actual name. I'd given up the battle and gone with it. My actual mother, who also wanted to be called Mom, snickered at my commentary.

It amazed me that my parents had made the journey all the way from Andromeda to witness me wed a man I'd plucked out of space.

"That's really not how flower girls are supposed to work, but frankly, this is so much cuter, this is how the tradition should have been," my mother announced. "Flower girls, on Earth, threw flowers. That's all. A little boy tended to be the ring bearer. I'm guessing you just saw flower girl and ring bearer in the listing?"

We had, and rather than try to cover up our amusing mistake, I nodded. "Well, we tried."

"This is so much better, but if you want to mimic a human ceremony, bring that little boy this girl likes and have them just walk together down the aisle. It'll be trivial to deck him out in flowers."

Delta's father took the hint and went off to secure our impromptu ring bearer.

"Anything else we've gotten woefully wrong, Mom?"

"Everything, but I love it and think this is perfect. Well, perfect for you. You never liked doing anything the easy or sensible way. When we'd been asked if we'd wanted to modify you, I'd thought your father had been out of his mind to request survival adaptations. But as I wanted you to live a long and happy life, I figured he'd been right. Now you're living among…"

"Feathered murder machines," I provided.

Mystoran, who'd been assigned as Delta's right hand Veloc for the wedding, hooted his laughter. "And you are our prized furred murder machine." And without missing a beat, he regaled my mother about how I'd slapped a tracker onto a bastard of a hatchling kidnapper and shot him out of a tree.

Miracle of a Lost Crimson Star pressed her head against my stomach, and I smiled at her, stroking my hand over her crest, careful to avoid her new decorations. "Still Water Under a Bridge will be with you, so you don't have to worry about how long it is until you can see him. The ceremony won't be that long, but you two will need to be quiet like we discussed."

She pressed closer to me and cooed.

Delta's father returned with Miracle Star's favorite friend, and the pair cooed at each other, nuzzled, and settled into their routine of greeting each other, preening their feathers, and otherwise drawing attention to themselves. "My son is growing rather impatient, as he seems convinced you're going to run straight for your ship and flee the planet rather than get married."

I gestured to my head, which sported a fortune in shiftgem crystals. "Part of my life support system is decorating my hair. I can't fly without a life support system." In reality, my life support system had been torn apart by an overenthusiastic Delta, who owed me a new one and had dealt with several hours of me crying over its destruction, however accidental. And by accidental, I suspected he'd been clumsy on purpose to make sure I couldn't flee the planet. "And part of my life support system is decorating my hair because *he broke it.*"

"And he's helping you fix it, just after the wedding. I don't know why he's so convinced you're going to run so he has to chase you."

I shrugged. "It's probably because I kept threatening to run off and take the impressionable hatchlings with me, training them to venture among the stars rather than stay on land. I even promised to bring the impressionable hatchlings back *and* get their parents' permission to take them off on short flights. I think he broke my life support system so I wouldn't actually do it."

"If he thinks that's going to stop you, he's crazier than I thought," his father muttered. "We need to get in our positions. Remember, no inciting the clans to battle each other until *later.*"

"Should I be concerned?" my mother asked.

"Only if you don't like watching feathered murder machines posture," I replied. "It's fun. They'll feed us while they posture, and if you're unlucky, you'll be adopted. If you're really unlucky, several clans will fight for the right to adopt you. They are not clear on how adoption actually works. Honestly, you're going to be adopted. You haven't run away screaming yet. You should have seen the technicians who came trying to rig up a new ship for the Cremora Deltans."

"It helped they sent the hatchlings out to greet us at the landport," my mother admitted. "We hadn't learned even the hatchlings are predators."

"They're adorable, and that gets them close enough to take no prisoners. It's too late for us all." I looked around the reception room that had been transformed into the pre-ceremony bridal suite. "Someone ran off with our foxes again."

"They're with Delta, and they're decked out in a ridiculous number of jewels. I'd been meaning to ask. Where did you get the male? He's an excellent specimen."

"I don't know where Carthello got him."

"The tentacle man with scales and claws?" my mother asked.

Right. Carthello had come for the wedding, citing the life-debt and a refusal to miss out on a day I was *forced* to accept gifts. "Yes, him. He's a good sort. He helped me acquire my stasis machine."

"We are rolling in kits, so I'll speak to him. They need good homes."

Oh, boy. My mother would end up becoming a black market supplier if given a chance—and she would specialize in having *vulpes vulpes* take over the universe. "Just don't forget the survivability mods. They need them in space."

"Yes, yes. We've been working on it. Ah, that reminds me. We'd like to tweak Pandora and her beau a little. We brought the machine, and we can test if they're compatible. I believe they are."

"What tweaks?" I demanded, narrowing my eyes.

"We've figured out how to reset their aging markers in

their DNA, so we can extend their lives to be roughly sixty Earth years. That's the longest we can manage without damaging quality of life. The older test subjects, who are from the generational ship, stay in the prime of life until dying of natural causes, typically heart attacks. We can't stop elements of aging in them, but we've unlocked the key we've wanted. To keep them for our lives, and that they won't suffer from old age like we will."

"It stops arthritis?"

"None of them we've modded have suffered arthritis."

"After the ceremony," I said, kissing my mother's cheek. "But thank you. Pandora means the world to me."

"We know. We've known since the moment you laid eyes on her and realized she was yours. From that moment, we knew you would do anything for her, and she's a smart fox. She knows it, too. Now, prepare yourself. I've been warned there will be a great deal of keening from the Veloc, who simply live for but cannot handle weddings. It will be chaos."

MY MOTHER'S prediction proved to be true, and I understood why there hadn't been any music for the wedding. Why bother with music with the keening, trilling, and cooing of the Veloc in the audience? Miracle of a Lost Crimson Star and Still Water Under a Bridge led the procession, and the pair bobbed their flower-decorated heads, adding to the cacophony with their hooted laughs.

At least they found the situation funny. I wanted to roll my eyes at the drama, but I focused on a rather nervous

Delta who seemed ready to take flight without the help of a spaceship.

Thanks to the oddity of Veloc ways, I had a collection of six fathers accompanying me, including Delta's, adding to the insanity. As I wasn't telling a Veloc he couldn't play father to a clan adoptee, I went along with it, and I'd even managed to arrange it so everyone got an equal share of attention.

The mothers had congregated near Delta, and I had no idea what their purpose in the ceremony was beyond to keep the men in line. Everyone paired up as planned, and I joined Delta in front of the crowd, which mostly consisted of the Veloc clans, black market operators, and a handful of other sentients who'd traveled across the universe to witness me wed one of my rescues.

It took about three minutes to realize the vows and sermon were formalities, not that anyone could hear them over the Veloc determined to notify the entire planet of a wedding. I only understood when I was to give my vow to Delta and accept his vow in return when the leader of the wedding, a rather old Veloc with gray feathers, claimed the rings from Miracle of a Lost Crimson Star and handed them over and clipped our marriage crystals, rainbow black shiftgem crystals, into our hair in the Veloc tradition.

The Veloc roared their approval, and I expected to suffer from ringing ears for a few days.

As the Veloc didn't kiss, not in the way humans did, we'd agreed we'd save more intimate displays of affection for a later time, opting to press our foreheads together, much like the Veloc did when showing another respect. We lacked crests, but it got the point across.

My husband chuckled at the insanity of it all, and once

we'd held the position for the appropriate time, he leaned forward to say, "Now you can run away if you'd like."

"Not without a spaceship I can't," I complained. "You broke my *life support system.*"

He laughed, turned to the crowd, and offered his arm to me, which I took. "So I did. Now we have to survive a gauntlet of keening Veloc. We now get to venture to my favorite part of the day."

"The presents?" I guessed.

"The presents," he confirmed in his most serious tone. "I have been promised *many* presents, and there's only one thing better than a present, and that's two presents."

Well, at least Delta made it easy to know what he liked. "I have a present for you you'll really like later."

"Oh?"

"Me naked in our bed."

SOMEHOW, we survived through an entire afternoon of presents. No matter what I said, the Veloc took the idea of life-debts seriously, which meant I needed to accept something from every single one of them who believed they owed me. To my dismay, the entire planet felt the same way.

"Why?" I wailed in one of the lulls of gift giving.

Mystoran, who'd taken on the role of registering every gift given, laughed at my misfortune. "You performed a miracle, that's why. Sure, the black market operators claimed her back, but you were the one who returned her. Of all the hatchlings stolen, she is the first to have made it home as a hatchling. The others? If they survive, they are several decades older, living enslaved until fighting for their freedom. Several clans have suffered from the loss of a hatchling this way. Some of the gifts you were given are from stolen hatchlings who didn't have someone to save them. You were but one piece of the working that brought Miracle Star home, but you were the most important part. Without you, she may not have made it home at all."

"Carthello would have done his best."

"He is toxic for our kind, and he would have killed her trying. That is why he wears unique clothes. A safety modification. You were her only hope. No one else at that spacestation could have cared for her. They were all adapted. It was good fortune. We learned of why she was in her condition from him. She'd been trying to feed herself because they couldn't feed her. They would have poisoned her trying. And she would have starved to death because she is too young—and the space station itself was dying," Mystoran explained.

"And things become clearer," I whispered, staring at the ridiculous number of gifts, many still wrapped, we would need to contend with before we could leave the planet. "I had no idea."

"If it appeases you a little, they appreciate how much you fight the life-debt. They understand you would have done it for any other hatchling without care for a reward. And we heard you didn't even bother checking your compensation for pulling your husband out of the fire."

I snorted and pointed at Delta. "He *is* my compensation. The tokens were paid out in advance to cover his feeding bill."

My husband laughed. "I can live with that. I have a present for you. As it seems the zealous Veloc have given us a break, shall we go see your present? It's a short trip, but we'll have a hover to get us there. We cannot risk your dress. That dress is a work of art, and we aren't allowed to destroy it until this evening. Then it's to be reduced to scraps. I'm not sure *why*, but when a Veloc tells me I have to shred your dress getting you out of it, I'm not going to argue."

I pointed at Mystoran's capped claws. "I'm guessing the Veloc wear dresses or some form of covering for their weddings, and they delight in shredding them while freeing their brides."

"It's a good guess. It's also true," Mystoran confirmed.

Well, I wouldn't miss the dress, and there would be plenty of pictures of me in it if I wanted to revisit the past. "Let's go see this present. Your present is forgiveness for trashing my life support system to make certain I wouldn't flee the planet before the wedding."

"That's a pretty good present," he admitted, getting to his feet and holding his hand out to me. "I'm just glad I didn't damage the crystals. I'm not sure why you're *wearing* your life support crystals, but I figure you're not going to lose them that way."

"One of the Veloc saw me with them and stole them, promising I'd have them back later. Maybe they thought they were one of the bazillion shiftgem crystals I now own? I'm going to need a nest on two planets to hold my entire collection."

"That you will. Now, close your eyes. I'll guide you, but I really want this to be a surprise."

As he hadn't asked much of me beyond forgiveness for breaking my life support system, I went along with his request and closed my eyes. "I'll miss you if you ruin my dress and get eaten by angry Veloc."

Mystoran hooted his amusement. "Just this once, I'll protect him."

"OKAY. YOU CAN OPEN YOUR EYES."

I obeyed, and the visitor landport of Veloci Minor surrounded us. "I see we have traveled quite a far distance of perhaps a kilometer to reach our destination."

"There was no way in hell I was asking you to walk that far in those shoes."

"And just like that, you reminded me why I decided it was a good idea to marry you. So deliciously practical."

Delta laughed, and he pointed at a nearby flight pad with a mid-ranged, long-distance interceptor with an extended body, likely a cargo bay. "I took your advice and challenged the Veloc clans to design the perfect spaceship for your needs. Now is the time where I will confess I was under strict orders by several Veloc that I would damage your life support system so they could replace it and add some special modifications to your ship."

Okay. In his shoes, I would have broken my life support system, too. "I still forgive you." I blinked at the ship, which was twice the size of mine. "You got me an *entire ship*?"

"Honestly, the Veloc are giving you the ship. I'm just claiming credit. I fed them intel every time we browsed the newest toys on the market. Breaking the life support system meant they could overhaul it while I kept you busy with the wedding. I do have some bad news for you, though."

There was bad news? They'd gotten me an entire new ship. I spluttered and pointed and the sleek beauty begging me to put her through her paces. "How can anything about this be *bad*?"

"Your life support system, your communication system, your engine, and your spare engine were overhauled. The overhaul is in pieces in your original ship, which is parked on the other side of your new ship. If you want to whisk me away to explore space, you're going to have to put it all back together again. Oh, and the bunks in your ship were completely redesigned, as I refuse to sleep on some tiny cot when I could have luxury accommodations with my wife."

Ah. I understood. Someone had given himself a wedding present. "I suppose I'll survive through the horribly tedious process of helping my husband put my spaceship together. One of us is going to like this more than the other."

"I'm the one who is going to like this more than the other."

"Like hell you are!" I shot him a glare and planted my hands on my hips. "That's *my* ship, Delta. Mine."

His smile caught me off guard, and I blinked at him. He reached over and pressed his finger to my lips to keep me quiet. I cooperated, as I'd learned he had something truly important to say if he went to such lengths.

"I love everything about you. You shine when you're working with your ship, and you glow when you're gliding through the stars. No matter where we go or what we do, I know you will find happiness in those little things needed to keep a spaceship floating safely through space. That's your ship, but you're my future, and nothing brings me more joy than wondering where you'll take us next. Where you go, I will follow, until death do we part."

I kissed his finger. "Until death do we part, then."

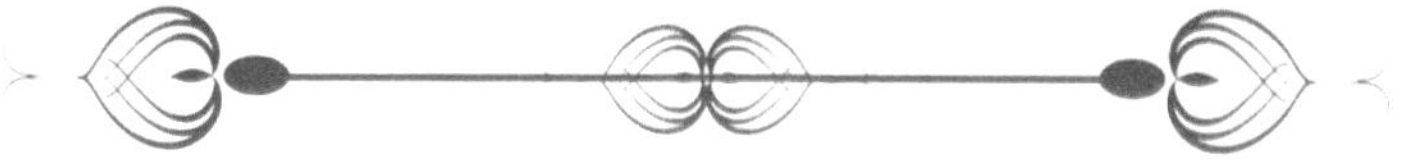

About the Author

RJ Blain suffers from a Moleskine journal obsession, a pen fixation, and a terrible tendency to pun without warning.

In her spare time, she daydreams about being a spy. Her contingency plan involves tying her best of enemies to spinning wheels and quoting James Bond villains until satisfied.

Bonus Story: Drastic Measures

Author's Note

I REALLY LOVE WRITING kidnapping stories, especially when the kidnapper is the spouse, partner, or associate of the kidnapped party. In this case, Viva is going to lose her mind if she stays on Cremora Delta 005-26.

This is meant as a slice of life for Viva and Delta after their first adventure together. As such, it's just a fun little romp.

There are errors, there are probably inconsistencies due to doing this solely for fun, and please don't ask me where this fits into the grand scheme of the upcoming short novels (and full-length features) that are in the works.

I know nothing, I'm just typing the words and making some effort to proofread what I've written.

P.S.: Please walk away now if mistakes, errors, inconsistencies, etc. bother you. This is not the story for you. This is a bonus story, not a work of polished or refined art. This is a slice-of-life style, whatever, let's have fun kind of tale.

Enjoy!

Drastic Measures

IF I WANTED to escape Cremora Delta 005-26, several things needed to happen. First, I needed to smuggle our foxes on board the ship without my husband being aware of my furry theft.

Delta adored his precious Boo-Boo, and life without Boo-Boo was terrible. The only time my husband pitched a worse fit was when I wandered off without him, as life without me underfoot was worse than terrible.

Where Delta went, Boo-Boo followed, much like Pandora tended to follow me around. Unlike Pandora, Boo-Boo tended to have a temper tantrum upon separation from his beloved human.

Fortunately for my sanity, Boo-Boo adored Pandora, so as long as I had my fox with me, I could get the spoiled rotten little brat to cooperate.

We made quite the family, where we chased each other in a relentless quest for attention.

I still questioned how the *vulpes vulpes* had ended up with the name of Boo-Boo, but it had something to do with how Delta cooed at his precious fluffball. Had I been wise, I would have named the fox something else, rather than waiting to see more of his personality, but no.

We had a fox named Boo-Boo, and I only had myself to blame for it.

Armed with my little girl and Boo-Boo's harness and leash, I waited for my spouse to go into a meeting he couldn't take us into and stole the animal from my father-in-law, who had been in the process of handing him off to my mother-in-law.

"What are you up to?" he asked, and the way he raised a brow indicated he expected an honest answer out of me.

I offered him a folded slip of paper. "I am holding myself and our foxes ransom, and he will have to come to a shady spaceport should he wish to pay said ransom. At that point, he will be kidnapped, and I will cart him off to do with as I please for a few weeks. Do act appropriately horrified your furry grandchildren have been petnapped."

My mother-in-law's laughter rang out. "How are you getting off planet this time?"

The first time I'd fled the planet to get back into space, during the outfitting of my ships, I'd created an incident. My Veloc conspirators had enjoyed every minute of the chase, as the Deltans learned how to venture into space to reclaim what was theirs.

Delta had led the charge, and I'd spent a solid week laughing at my spouse's antics.

Once again, the Veloc had come to the rescue, sparing me from being trapped on the planet. "I made use of one of those pesky life-debts to summon a ship, claiming insufficient romancing due to meetings. If I want any romancing, I have to be taken from this world, else the meetings win."

That got my father-in-law laughing, too. "You planned your own kidnapping so you can, in turn, kidnap Delta?"

"He's obviously been overworking, and I couldn't help

but notice he mystically had an entire month of clean schedule manifest last week." The clean schedule had prompted my immediate contact with the Veloc, who'd arrived on the planet via the most direct route, ready to cart me off the instant I could escape with our foxes. "If you hadn't wanted him to be kidnapped, you wouldn't have given me an entire month to work with."

My father-in-law checked the ransom note and snickered at my piddly demands. "I see you want to upgrade your living quarters on your ship again."

One day, the ship that Delta had given me for our wedding would be perfection, but first, I needed to do a few more modifications. At the questionable spaceport, I could acquire the parts I needed. "Pandora and Boo-Boo need more space."

Pandora and Boo-Boo always needed more space, and I had plans for more safety cages for them installed in key points throughout the ship, which could also be used to stow other rescued animals as we came across them.

Boo-Boo squeaked upon hearing his name, and I took the time to pet the fox and praise him for being a good boy. With luck, he wouldn't indulge in his typical separation anxiety, although I expected it.

Delta had done a good job of charming us all.

"I will do you a favor and put together a proper ransom, and I will even add an entry to the black market, thus ridding you of yet another life-debt you don't want. I'm sure your various operator friends would love to play the game. I take it you're testing Delta's ability to handle the ship alone?"

As Delta had six months under his belt with his shiny new piloting license but no solo flights, there was little better way to get him ready for the big leagues than to send him off in our ship on a short but easy flight.

The smuggler's port could be reached in five hours by a determined pilot willing to do two gate hops.

Delta could handle both hops, and if he needed help docking with the port, he could be tethered and towed in as needed.

"Somewhat. Mostly, if I don't get into space, I will go mad. But testing his new license on his first solo flight is good, too. The port is equipped with tows and tethers if he struggles with parking the ship."

"We'll delay him for a few hours so you can get a head start, enforce his mandatory rest period before he can pilot, and send him after you in the morning. Tell the cousins we said hello and have a good time. If you're planning on breeding your foxes, swing by Veloci Minor. It's their breeding season for foxes."

I read between the lines; my in-laws wanted foxes, too. "Boo-Boo is old enough now, and I have no problem with accidentally forgetting to give the foxes medications." That someone had developed a safe birth control for *vulpes vulpes* amused me—and it helped mitigate some of the more troublesome fox behaviors, especially in space. "Oh, woe is me. I am being kidnapped. I simply won't have time to go back to our quarters to retrieve that box."

"I'll send your parents a message warning them you are up to your usual tricks," Delta's father promised. "I'll cover your back. I can't promise that won't buy you more time than until morning, but I'm sure you can make do."

I encouraged both foxes to follow me, waved, and fled in the direction of the spaceport.

SEVEN HOURS after departing Cremora Delta 005-26, we arrived at the spaceport owned and operated by the black market. The Veloc entered through the exports section, received preferential treatment destined to draw unwanted attention, and docked at an indoor bay meant for a much larger vessel. I monitored the conditions of the bay until it registered as safe for life before retrieving my foxes, putting them in their suits to keep up with their training, and bouncing down the ramp.

Carthello met us, and he'd added a set of horns to his shape since the last time I'd seen him. The horns, curved like a ram's, reminded me of a mythological beast from Earth's folklore. "Horns?"

"Purely decorative in nature. I was feeling fancy. How are you?"

"Now that I'm off that planet for a while, great! I need parts, Carthello. I need parts, and I have Veloc willing to carry them for me."

"You had your own father-in-law put out a bounty for you, anonymously, with a set ransom for your safe return. And the old bastard had the audacity to claim you were calling in a life-debt for it."

I stared into a set of Carthello's many eyes, grinned, and replied, "One of you assholes gets to be set free from a life-debt to play along with my father-in-law, who cut my husband free for an *entire month.*"

Unable to help myself, I whipped my tail back and forth,

much like my foxes when they were at their peak level of excitement.

Carthello laughed at me. "All right, all right. It's clear you needed some time in space. What upgrades are you after?"

"I need cages for the foxes that can be installed in the niches around the ship. I'll use them for other animals being transported, too, but I don't have a set in every sector yet, and I want them. After I've kidnapped Delta, I'm taking him to Veloci Minor and breeding the foxes. The in-laws want kits."

"You'll want the genetic mods for them, too."

"Especially the ones for their scent glands," I replied.

Pandora and Boo-Boo had both come already modded to be less offensive to the noses of delicate sentients, but a few visits to Veloci Minor had taught me the truth about most foxes.

Foxes *stank*. No, they reeked. They could clear a room just from existing, the stench so putrid it could turn my stomach for hours afterwards.

My kits would be modded to spare our noses shortly before Pandora would give birth, and they'd all have their survival and longevity mods done so they could be beloved pets. I would also acquire foxes from a different line, have them modded, and gift all the babies in breeding pairs along with the medications and treatments needed to control their populations and keep them happy.

Vulpes vulpes would one day rule Cremora Delta 005-26.

"Easily done. I'm sure you can eliminate at least three life-debts with the work, and Delta might even praise you for sparing his wallet for a change." Carthello waved a tentacle, indicating I should follow him. He guided me through the spaceport, and my escort of Emerald Crest Veloc trailed behind me, reminding me of oversized, lethal ducklings. "I have brought out a lovely cage for you to trap your man in. I want to test a new holograph system that should duplicate your image live into the cage. The instant he goes to set you free, he will be the one trapped."

Ah, I loved the shady black market operators. Ever since legalizing some of their activities, they'd become rather fun, toeing the line with glee and testing new technology for the joy of discovery. "Can you demonstrate some of your new restraints? To make it look particularly realistic?"

"I have a nice little toy he will freak out over if he sees you wearing it, especially if you should don some nice lingerie."

The black market operators must have gone shopping on my behalf again, and I laughed. "Mystoran? I'm going to need you to help with my baubles," I stated, and as the Veloc liked when *homo sapiens* got uppity with them, I placed my hands on my hips and dared the predator to defy me.

The Veloc bounded over, and his emerald crest snapped up. "Are you planning on some romancing?"

"I am planning on wearing as little as possible while being bejeweled to be presented as a captive prize. In reality, it's a ruse to trick your little cousin into thinking I'm about to be sold into slavery. We're going to test a cage on him, and I will be performing my kidnapping of his person while wearing practically nothing." I turned my attention to Carthello. "I'm going to need a shower, and I'm going to raid your stash of feminine care products so I smell as good as I look. If I'm going to play this part, I want to be so damned gorgeous he forgets he's capable of speaking."

"I believe she would like some romancing," Mystoran

stated, and he bobbed his upper body in the black market operator's direction, careful to stay out of touching range.

Carthello's modifications would make a mess of my day, as I'd learned it took weeks for a Veloc to recover from the hellish toxin he exuded. In good news for Mystoran, if an accident happened, we had two or so hours to administer the antidote, and Carthello always carried a few doses with him just in case. "I'd like some romancing, along with a few weeks in space and long enough on Veloci Minor to breed our foxes and let them have a good time. We may go spend some time alone in space while the foxes have themselves a good time on Veloci Minor."

"Ah, you wish for kits."

I could read into his statement more than one way, and I answered him with a shrug.

Delta and I would get around to having children eventually. My survivability modifications would extend my fertility for decades, and I expected Delta would end up modified as well.

His people loved him, and a modified leader stayed a leader longer.

But before I worried about that, I had a kidnapping to perform, romancing to enjoy, and mischief to accomplish. "My in-laws wish for kits, desperately, and Boo-Boo is old enough now to handle his fatherly duties with grace."

Carthello snorted. "I still can't believe you let your husband name that poor fox Boo-Boo."

Boo-Boo, who adored Carthello, whipped his hindquarters in excitement. Fortunately for my sanity, his various defense mechanisms did not bother the fox, although Carthello took care with praising the fox and how he petted the animal.

"My tendency to avoid naming things backfired spectacularly. Now I have a husband I named Delta, because he's a Deltan, and a fox named Boo-Boo because I waited too long to give him a dignified name. I'm going to just name the kits so my husband doesn't."

"Wisdom grows in mysterious ways," the black market operator teased. He led me deep into the spaceport to a security room. "We're going to test our new cage and holograph system on this lovely lady and her husband. We have been granted permission to dress her appropriately. Someone get her a proper bathing kit, the Veloc will handle her adornments, and you lot can fight over which set of lingerie she'll wear. Leave some mystery. The buyer doesn't want everything exposed from the start, after all. But do be scandalous. That's half the fun. Get the decorative chain set to add some spice to our display. Make sure the cameras are all working, because we will regret it if we don't capture every moment of his on video."

THE RESTRAINTS, made of precious metals and jewels, went well with the elaborate hairstyle the Veloc concocted, transforming me into a living work of art. To make it worth my while, we'd wasted some time doing a complete photoshoot, and I'd had a blast taking pictures with the Veloc, Carthello, and the ridiculous number of black market operators, smugglers, and others convinced they owed me a life-debt.

To make the scene even more offensive to my husband, who'd lose his mind upon seeing the scene, Pandora and

Boo-Boo were also kitted up in jewels, a harness, and decorative restraints that did absolutely nothing to hamper the *vulpes vulpes*. Fortunately, the promise of treats and a visit with their daddy convinced both animals to play along.

The holograph recording process took an hour to set up, and we received word my ship approached twenty minutes after finishing all our preparations. Just in case the live-streaming holograph failed to function, we'd recorded ten minutes of me playing at being a forlorn and sad fox, with drooped ears and a despondent expression.

I didn't do despondent all that well, but a threat of keeping Boo-Boo and Pandora for three months if I couldn't get my face to cooperate did the trick.

As I'd taught him, Delta docked on the imports side of the spaceport, and the various operators in on the scheme made it so he could only access the hallways and rooms leading to the trap, the cage meant for live captures of most sentients, even Veloc.

I struggled with my act, but Pandora and Boo-Boo settled into their roles with admirable grace, whining their distress and doing every single behavior I trained them not to do when upset over something.

As I'd worked with Delta on how to keep our pets from driving us insane, he'd fall for their trickery hook, line, and sinker.

The promised recording played in my view, and Delta abandoned all common sense and went straight for the holograph decoy without even a moment of hesitation. Once trapped, the holograph vanished, and I broke down in a fit of laughter. As the cage was set up a short distance away, I hopped to my feet, gathered up the chain, and hurried on over to observe my spouse come to terms with his captivity in person.

The foxes followed, and they gave into their excitement and glee, yipping and bouncing around me with zero cares in the world.

While I favored Delta with my best smile, he scowled. "You are the most evil wife in the *entire universe*, Viva!"

Ah, I loved the sound of true praise. It warmed my soul and brought me endless joy. "You can thank your parents later." As the lingerie set did an excellent job of creating a vast valley of cleavage, I leaned his way to enhance his view. "I have three sets."

My murmured words captured his attention completely, and he spent a rather long time admiring me from head to toe. When it clicked I'd tricked him into piloting solo, he narrowed his eyes. "You just wanted me to bring the ship here alone."

I allowed myself a smug smile. "Yes. You need the practice. Your parents helpfully cleared your schedule, so I have arranged for you to be my captive prize."

"I suppose I should be grateful you didn't make me stew in this cage for long."

I nodded. "Of course, you probably would have heard me laughing. Do you know how hard it is to act like I've been dressed up for sale on the market? Boo-Boo did a better job of acting sad than I did."

"Had I taken a chance to actually look at you, I might have noticed something amiss, but I seem to have abandoned all sense."

My Veloc conspirators joined us, and they hooted and whistled their amusement, setting my husband free from the cage. Mystoran nuzzled his little cousin and said, "They wanted to test if the holographs could work as bait with the cage, and that the cage worked as intended." I snagged the collar and leash we'd selected for my husband, and I secured it around his throat.

Like our foxes, I failed to resist the urge to swish my tail over my successful acquisition of my spouse.

Delta raised a brow. "Is there something you're trying to tell me, Viva?"

"No, but there's plenty I plan on showing you in the comfort of our quarters while we adventure through space."

"But what about the ransom?"

I leered at him.

"You are such a naughty fox, Viva."

Yes, I was, and I looked forward to spending the next few weeks in space proving that to him.

www.ingramcontent.com/pod-product-compliance
Lightning Source LLC
Chambersburg PA
CBHW020502310726
48979CB00016B/2759/J

* 9 7 8 1 6 4 9 6 4 1 3 9 7 *